P9-CSC-505

LONE RANGER

The Texas Ranger was alone in the lawless border town, with a slug in his shoulder and his quarry closing in for the kill.

Suddenly a hot round caught the would-be killer below his right armpit and ripped through both lungs. At once the backup men in the alley reacted.

"What th'hell?" one blurted. He raised the rifle he held to his shoulder.

O'Grady stepped from the shadows and shot him in the gut. Then he sighted in on the leader, Ballard. The outlaw squealed like a pig when a bullet splintered his shoulder. The last gunman raised his rifle. Canyon cocked his Colt. "Don't," he said simply.

O'Grady was heading south of the border after Colonel Death. But this trip would have a lot of bloody detours. . . .

CANYON O'GRADY RIDES ON

CANYON O'GRADY

14

COLONEL
DEATH

by
Jon Sharpe

A SIGNET BOOK

SIGNET
Published by the Penguin Group
Penguin Books USA Inc., 375 Hudson Street,
New York, New York 10014, U.S.A.
Penguin Books Ltd, 27 Wrights Lane,
London W8 5TZ, England
Penguin Books Australia Ltd, Ringwood,
Victoria, Australia
Penguin Books Canada Ltd, 2801 John Street,
Markham, Ontario, Canada L3R 1B4
Penguin Books (N.Z.) Ltd, 182–190 Wairau Road,
Auckland 10, New Zealand

Penguin Books Ltd, Registered Offices:
Harmondsworth, Middlesex, England

First published by Signet, an imprint of New American Library,
a division of Penguin Books USA Inc.

First Printing, July, 1991
10 9 8 7 6 5 4 3 2 1

 REGISTERED TRADEMARK—MARCA REGISTRADA

Printed in the United States of America

PUBLISHER'S NOTE
This is a work of fiction. Names, characters, places, and incidents either
are the product of the author's imagination or are used fictitiously, and any
resemblance to actual persons, living or dead, events, or locales is entirely
coincidental.

Canyon O'Grady

His was a heritage of blackguards and poets, fighters and lovers, men who could draw a pistol and bed a lass with the same ease.

Freedom was a cry seared into Canyon O'Grady, justice a banner of his heart.

With the great wave of those who fled to America, the new land of hope and heartbreak, solace and savagery, he came to ride the untamed wildness of the Old West.

With a smile or a six-gun, Canyon O'Grady became a name feared by some and welcomed by others, but remembered by all . . .

Texas, 1868, where the land was as big and wide as a madman's ambition . . .

1

Hot, dry wind blew across the desertlike terrain of southwest Texas, whipping around twenty-five men who sat on their horses in loose formation. Here and there white-and-red swaths signified wounds. More than twenty bodies littered the ground, sprawled in grotesque positions. Flames crackled behind the survivors and added to their thirst and the discomfort of powder-grimed faces. Their blue uniforms and kepis represented a variety of branches of service: infantry blue, artillery red, cavalry yellow. In a line before them stood their NCOs and officers, all facing a single man.

Although not tall, barely making five-nine, nor broadshouldered, he had a commanding quality that riveted the attention of the soldiers he addressed. "Men, from this day forward, we can rely only upon ourselves. It took a long time for me to arrange transfers for all of you to my command. I did it because each and every one of you has special skills necessary to our current campaign. You wouldn't be here if you didn't measure up. As with Caesar in ages past, today we have crossed our Rubicon. There will be no turning back." He removed his blue garrison hat with the goldbraid headband and let the sear breeze ruffle his thick, grayshot black hair.

"Some of you are not accomplished horsemen. I will expect you to familiarize yourself with the evolutions of mounted drill, the nomenclature of your tack and saddle, and your animal's habits within seventy-two hours. As to your introduction to riding technique, you have my sincerest sympathy. George McClellan may have had his headquarters in the saddle he designed and foisted off on the army, but it was his backside that took the punishment."

"You tell 'em, Jud," a barrellike sergeant shouted through a guffaw.

"Now, Captain Means and the other officers, including

my son, Edward, are capable leaders. Likewise, Sergeants
Nally, Gruber, and Nimms and the other noncoms are wise
in the ways of battle. You will obey their orders unquestion-
ably. We can no longer wait for the enemy to come to us.
We will carry the fight to them. If each of you performs to
the best of his ability, I can promise you success. And with
it, wealth beyond the boldest imagination. After today there
is no turning back.

"Where you find danger, I will be there also. Where you
find glory, I shall praise you. We will meet adversity
together and vanquish it. Remember this, you are the best,
if some of the most cantankerous, soldiers ever spawned by
the United States Army. I'm proud to lead you on to this
adventure.

"Now, you know how I feel. Adjutant, form the troops
in a column of twos to the left."

"Sir! Company, attenshun! Form column of twos to the
left . . . Ho-o-o!"

Far from precise, the troops gigged and goaded their
mounts into a rough semblance of a double column. From
inside his blue tunic, which bore the epaulets of a full colonel, Judson Kilgore took a strictly nonregulation black
ostrich plume and affixed it on one side of his broad-
brimmed hat, creasing the tightly woven felt and fastening
it alongside the crown with a silver pin. He then walked his
horse to the head of the column and raised his right hand.

"Forward, at the trot . . . Ho-o-oo!"

With jerks and starts, the company moved out at irregular
intervals. Behind them they left the sprawled corpses of the
soldiers they had murdered, and the burning palisades and
buildings of Camp Fenton, Department of Texas, United
States Army.

Located on Scott Circle in Washington City, the Daniel
Webster Hotel catered to an above-average class of visitor.
Its top two floors boasted "refined suites of unsurpassed
quality." In the parlor of one of these two-room accommodations, an overlarge copper hip tub occupied the major
portion of the floor space.

In it sat a broad-shouldered, rawboned man of indetermi-
nate age, his large square-jawed head capped by thick waves
of flame-red hair. Foam-capped wavelets slopped over the
sides, driven by the energetic efforts of a shapely young

woman who stood behind the bather, wielding a brush. She wore an engaging smile and long, glossy dun tresses done in sausage curls. Otherwise she was as bare as the day she came into the world.

"Ah, Moira, that's a wonderful service you're performing," Canyon O'Grady declared with a relaxed sigh. "I've not felt this relaxed in a long time."

A titter of laughter came from the lovely young woman as she bent forward and saw the obvious result of her attentions. "I wouldn't say you were all that relaxed. You certainly weren't last night." She shifted the position of the brush and bore in.

O'Grady laughed, a deep, throaty sound. "Wasn't I, now? Maybe they don't teach young girls everything they should back in Ireland."

"Devil take you, Canyon O'Grady, we've been American since back before the Revolution. My great-grandfather, Seamus, was one of Sam Adams' Sons of Liberty."

"Good for him! Now, be a good girl and move a bit to the right. There, good. Aaaah, that's how a man should always have a bath."

"What's this important business that brings you to Washington, Canyon, dear?"

O'Grady frowned. For no reason could he reveal his special commission as a government agent who worked under the direct supervision and authorization of the President of the United States. He shrugged, and evaded.

"Politics. Isn't that what brings everyone here?"

Perky, pink, and nude Moira Quinn squinched her face into gullied lines of disbelief. "Somehow, you don't strike me as a typical politician. You aren't oily enough."

"Now, that's a sad commentary on the times," O'Grady offered in hopes of keeping the mood light.

Ignoring his remark, Moira pursued her fantasy. "I see you more as an engineer, laying out and building one of the great railroads in the West."

"Isn't gaining grants of right-of-way a matter of politics?" he inquired as he reached up and tweaked one full, firm, globular breast.

Moira squeaked in appreciation. She bent low, brushed his shoulders with erect dark red nipples. O'Grady's other hand found her silken thigh and traced the outer lines of it to her nicely rounded rump. Moira shivered with anticipation.

O'Grady's long, work-hardened fingers tiptoed across yielding flesh to her swollen mound. A thick chestnut mat covered her cleft, which O'Grady parted before advancing. Moira sighed.

Slowly O'Grady's digits traced the vertical aperture, moistened by her ready flow. He located the sensitive node at the apex and massaged it energetically. Moira began to sway and utter small sounds of pleasure. When her vocal appreciation changed to a whimper, he withdrew and plunged inward along the main channel.

"Aye! Oh, my. My, yes," Moira approved.

"After last night you have something left over for now?" O'Grady asked playfully.

"After last night, I'd die if *you* didn't," she gasped. Moira struggled for control over her runaway body. "There, now, that should do you," she managed with only a hint of her growing arousal.

"How do I look?" O'Grady asked.

"I'll have to get around front to be sure," Moira told him.

She raised her shapely leg and swung it over his shoulder. O'Grady removed his exploring hand and looked upward at the font of his happiness. Her rich, feminine aroma made his head swirl. He took in the details until Moira swung the other limb forward and propelled herself to the front of the tub. She turned and found her gaze arrested by the upright shaft of his desire. She straddled his hips and bent low to kiss him.

O'Grady chuckled when her rigid nipples brushed his chest. A tuft of the same scarlet color at mid-line between round medallions of pectoral muscles caught Moira's attention and she twined a few strands around her finger while their lips met. She kissed openmouthed, urgent and demanding.

Their tongues flirted, darted, explored. Savoring her sweetness, O'Grady gently traced the line of her head, an ear, along her jawline with a strong, thick finger. He followed her throat to the indentation between collarbones and lingered a moment.

"You're a beautiful girl, and a good lover too," O'Grady informed her. "Reminds me of a snippet of Hugh O'Don-nell's. 'Over hills, and through dales,/ Have I roamed for your sake;/ All yesterday I sailed with sails/ On river and on lake./ The Erne, at its highest flood, I dashed across unseen,/ For there was lightning in my blood,/ My dark Rosaleen!/ My own Rosaleen!' There, what do you think?''

"I think you must have swallowed the Blarney Stone, Canyon O'Grady." She eased back, one hand exploring his belly, awash in the soapy water. Then she slid further and wrapped tapered fingers around his manhood. Slowly she began to stroke it. "*This* is poetry to me, Canyon sweetie."

A murmur of soft laughter rose in her throat. O'Grady saw the pulse throbbing there, thought it beauteous, and wished that he could bend words to suit him like Hugh O'Donnell. Her ministrations grew more strenuous.

Ripples of enjoyment ran through O'Grady's body. He watched her swaying, mesmerized by the rhythmic shift of her delightful breasts. A sudden impish thought brought a glow to his deep cobalt eyes.

"Are you ever going to get around to it?" he asked sharply. "The real thing, that is?"

Biting her lip to keep from laughing out loud, Moira adjusted her position until she straddled his hips, her darkly furred triangle poised above his upthrust member. Slowly she lowered herself. Anticipation flexed the hard plates of O'Grady's belly muscles. Moira edged closer.

Initial contact sent shivers through them at once. Aided by gravity, Moira let her wet and welcoming cleft part around the arrowhead of his maleness. With teasing languor it eased within the leafy portals. O'Grady sighed and fought to restrain himself enough to not rush her planned ensnarement.

Abruptly she allowed him to invade her a slight bit more. Contract and relax, and more of his pulsing shaft cleaved her seat of desire. Concentrating, she added a little more. A sigh that became a gasp accompanied the halfway mark. Restraint had all but marginally fled from O'Grady. He made ready to thrust upward in a spasm of desire and hilt himself.

And then someone knocked on the door.

"What the hell?" O'Grady roared in frustration.

"Someone knocked," Moira stated unnecessarily.

"Then find out who it is and send them the hell away."

"My, you're forceful today," Moira teased as she withdrew from the bath and reached for a wraparound dressing gown.

Enfolded in it, she dripped her way to the door. With a resentful twist of the knob she opened the portal to reveal a young messenger in a livery vaguely familiar. "Oh—ah—excuse me. I was looking for a Mr. Canyon O'Grady. Isn't this his suite?"

"It is, and I'm here, so come on in and stop babbling," O'Grady growled from the tub.

"A message, sir," the youth stammered.

"Obviously," O'Grady snapped tartly.

"I'm—ah—to wait for a reply, sir."

"Then do so over there," O'Grady demanded, pointing to the bow window that looked out on Massachusetts Avenue. Out of the copper tub and wrapped around the middle with a large, warm towel, O'Grady used a finger to break the blob of sealing wax. Unfolding the thick, all-rag, cream-colored paper, he silently read the message.

"The President of the United States requests the presence of Mr. Canyon O'Grady at the White House, at Mr. O'Grady's convenience. Use the Pennsylvania Avenue entrance."

At his convenience, eh? Coming from the President, that meant at once. "Tell the gentleman who sent this that I will be there promptly in one hour," he told the messenger, who nervously eyed O'Grady's big hands and broad shoulders. To Moira he said, "It's that business I was telling you about. Time and tide, as they say."

With a start that ended his ogling, the young man headed for the door. "Aren't you going to tip him, Canyon?"

Tip a member of the White House staff? O'Grady looked from Moira to the messenger. "Tip him? Whatever for?" Suddenly the idea amused him. He crossed to his trousers and fished out a quarter, which he flipped across the room in a high arc. "There you go. Be quick now."

"What about us?" Moira asked plaintively. "We were oh so close."

O'Grady gave her a look of genuine regret. "I'll be back. I promise. And when I come, I promise I'll love you till your eyes cross and your heart leaps into your throat."

"God, Canyon, you're so ro*mantic*."

Sunlight glinted off the wide, shallow expanse of water. Across the river, which the Mexicans called the Rio Bravo del Norte, distorting heat waves rose in shimmering columns from the desert terrain of the state of Chihuahua. After four days of hard riding, Colonel Kilgore had brought his band of deserters to the Rio Grande. The colonel relaxed in his saddle, Captain Lancelot Means beside him, in the shade of a paloverde tree.

Through a pair of field glasses he studied the far bank and the undulating land beyond. A few crows worried themselves in a cottonwood; age-worn footpaths led from ground level to the water's edge. To the left, some five hundred yards distant, the purpose of one of these became evident in the naked brown bodies of small boys splashing in the shallows. A single buzzard flew circular patrol over the scrub and cactus on the Chihuahua side. The country looked so blasted, desolate, hostile, that Judson Kilgore developed a momentary sense of hopelessness, even regret.

No, he steadied his resolve, they had forced him into this precipitate action. *They* had had it in for him from the start. The hazing that had taken on the aspect of harassment at West Point, the attitude of the instructors, the brutality of the upper classmen, the humiliation of placing thirty-fourth in a class of forty-two—all had been designed to put the upstart in his proper place. He knew that, believed it without question. To them, he was the nobody from Ohio, without the proper family ties, no influence in the War Department, no patronage, beyond the appointment, by the politicians. Then the assignments, all those postings that no one wanted. Each led to a worse one. And all the while the tisking and tusking by his superiors, the viciously wagging, slashing tongues of their wives. They had followed him from duty station to duty station.

Granted, his accomplishments during the Civil War had not been brilliant. How could they be? Not with the dregs of the Union Army assigned to his unit. He'd shown them, though. He had taken those brutish animals and turned them into soldiers. Some of them, including those with him at the present, had remained loyal to him for years, through even long separations. Judson Kilgore sighed and lowered the glasses.

"Well, there it is, Mexico."

Stale whiskey fumes scented Lancelot Means's breath as he issued a profound belch and spoke derisively. "Looks like the world's hottest, driest shithouse."

A fleeting frown put a deep vertical line between Judson Kilgore's thick bushy eyebrows. Lance Means's drinking had been responsible for his long time as a captain, more so than the haggling penny-pinchers of the War Department who had reduced the size of the army and frozen promotions for several years. Not that Lance couldn't hold his liquor—he could hold too damn much of it. Yet, drunk or sober, Colonel Kilgore had never seen a more competent or courageous company-grade officer in training or in combat.

"It's our destiny," Judson Kilgore contradicted.

Whiskey fumes filled the space between them again as Means hissed, "Bullshit."

"You and I have been committed to this for nearly a year, Lance."

"Some of the men have only been at Fenton for a matter of two weeks. Still, for some reason I cannot fathom, the troops are behind you."

"Thank you for that, at least, Lance. I know this is a large undertaking, a dangerous one. They're shaking down well. I think we're ready to cross now."

"I'll get right to it." Means turned in his saddle. "Sergeant Nimms, ready the men to cross the river."

"Yes, sir," Nimms responded with enthusiasm.

His zeal transmitted to the troopers as they splashed into the Rio Grande. They entered at a walk, spread out and increased to a trot, then a wild run. Tempestuous yells came from the men in line abreast as they waved their kepis and urged more speed from their mounts. Silvery sprays leapt neck-high as the horses increased their pace.

On the far shore the exuberance startled three men, who struggled with a heavy-laden wagon. One of them, José Urubia, glanced up and saw the blue-clad troops dashing toward their illegal load of whiskey and shouted to his companions.

"*¡Ten cuidado, amigos! Los soldados viene.*"

His friends instantly took flight, abandoning their cargo of contraband and scrambling up the steep bank toward the desert flats beyond. Sergeant Gruber spotted them first. He let out a shout and pointed a gauntleted hand in their direction.

"Over there, get those men," he bellowed.

Two troopers joined him and they quickly leapt ahead of the advancing line of yelling troopers. Sergeant Gruber gained ground rapidly and saw a terrified face looking back at him. He laughed, showing tobacco-yellowed teeth, and drove blunt cavalry spurs into his mount's ribs.

Straining to keep ahead of the charging soldiers, José glanced to his left and saw a trooper snatch Jorge Zamorra off his feet, a big gloved hand gripping the back of Jorge's white cotton shirt. To the other side José heard a shriek of surprise and pain as his second companion went sprawling, knocked off his feet by the broad front shoulder of a bay horse.

Once more José glanced behind him and saw a huge hand reaching for him. He tried desperately for more speed and failed. In the last second before he was yanked off his feet, José attempted to cut to one side. Then he knew the helplessness of capture.

"Who are these men?" Colonel Kilgore demanded when Sergeant Gruber and the two enlisted men rode up with their captives.

"Dunno, sir," Gruber answered.

Kilgore's eyes narrowed. "They might be spies for the Mexican Army."

"I doubt that, Father," Edward Kilgore called as he trotted up to the group on the bank.

His long black locks, glossy and heavy with pomade, bounced stiffly in the breeze under the wide brim of his officer's garrison hat. His pale complexion and watery eyes of an indistinct blue-gray-green hue gave him the appearance of a young man slowly recovering from a long illness. Thin, bloodless lips added to the illusion. Blame his mother for those looks, Judson Kilgore thought bitterly.

"What gives you that idea, Lieutenant?" Colonel Kilgore snapped.

"Their wagon is full of barrels of American whiskey. There are no Mexican tax stamps, so I'm certain they must be smugglers."

"Revenue runners, eh? Smugglers have often been employed as spies," the colonel opined.

"What'll we do with them, Colonel?" Sergeant Gruber asked.

Colonel Kilgore drew his Model '63 Remington service revolver from its flap holster and shot José low in the belly. Instantly Sergeant Gruber released his hold on the back of

the mortally wounded man's shirt. José sprawled in the
sandy dirt, twitching convulsively, and drew into a fetal ball.
"I think that answers your question, Sergeant Gruber.
Tend to the others and we'll move out."

Gruber exchanged glances with the two privates and drew
his own sidearm. While the commands rang out to form a
column of twos, the dull thuds of revolver fire at close range
shattered the midmorning air. Colonel Kilgore assumed his
position at the head of the column with a jaunty air and the
renegade troops rode away into the Chihuahua desert.

Behind them, José Urubia groaned mightily in his misery
and tried to frame a prayer. Blinking away sand and tears,
he looked up to see the muzzle of Sergeant Gruber's
revolver steady on his forehead. With a loud bang, José
Urubia gave up his soul and silence settled on the southern
bank of the Rio Grande.

2

President Andrew Johnson stood with his back to the room,
hands clasped behind him, staring out the tall floor-to-ceiling window of his office in the East Wing of the White
House. Across the well-tended lawn, which had only begun
to restore itself after years of neglect, he watched the constant stream of carriages and buggies along Pennsylvania
Avenue. The Treasury Building was to the east, his right,
and across the broad thoroughfare, Lafayette Park. A troubled frown creased his brow. He wore his gray hair long,
clubbed at the mid-ear line, his severely receded brow
deemphasized by this style. He turned when a discreet click
of the door latch announced the entry of his next
appointment.

"Welcome to the White House, Mr. O'Grady." The President spoke heartily. His frown deepened at O'Grady's
reply.

"It's not often I get the consideration of receiving my

orders in person. Usually some flunky hunts me down and gives them to me in the middle of nowhere."

Johnson's overlarge head and barrel chest robbed his considerable stature of the appearance of height. He indicated a chair and walked to his own behind a large rosewood desk. Dark mahogany paneling covered three walls, with a globe, coat tree, and a casual array of settees, wing chairs, and a low serving table the only other furniture.

"This is an important and highly sensitive matter, Mr. O'Grady. Since you were in Washington anyway, I felt it necessary to see you at once."

"If your expression is any indication, I'd say the entire Union is in danger."

"Not exactly, though close," Johnson informed him, his soft Tennessee burr deepening as he addressed the subject of their meeting. "Only yesterday I received most distressing news by telegraph from Texas. The Army Department of Texas, to be exact."

"Trouble with Mexico again?" O'Grady surmised.

"Not yet, and I hope to act quickly enough to prevent any. The gist of it is this. An officer of the United States Army, a field-grade officer, and an as yet unknown number of men have deserted their duty post and ridden off to the southwest. The report indicates that they have gone on a rampage of bloodshed and plunder."

O'Grady looked genuinely puzzled. "Where do I come in? The army has its own means of dealing with deserters."

"Granted. My information is that they may be heading into Mexico, where the army cannot follow them, and the possibility of an international incident is extremely likely. Besides which, before they departed, the officer involved, Colonel Judson Kilgore, and the men following him murdered the loyal members of the garrison and put Camp Fenton to the torch. They are wanted for murder, arson, destruction of government property, and desertion. Mr. William Evarts, my attorney general, suggests that it might also be possible to charge them with sedition."

"Again, why not use the army's resources?" O'Grady inquired with raised eyebrows.

"Secretary of State Seward was here early this morning. It is his opinion, and mine, that given the unbalanced personality of Judson Kilgore—his army records verified that—and the unstable conditions in Mexico following the ouster

of the French, and the slow pace of international recogni-
tion of the Juárez government, it might be possible that the
renegade colonel is set on an adventure in buccaneering.
Specifically, carving out a hunk of Mexico for himself.

"Before he can do that," the President went on, rubbing
a big square hand over his face as though to remove the
lines of worry and regret, "it is absolutely vital that he and
his renegades be stopped."

"A large order, Mr. President," O'Grady sighed. It
seemed he only got the tough ones, the cases others of the
small cadre of government agents wanted nothing to do
with. "Tell me about Kilgore."

"Judson Kilgore was in the class of 1845 at West Point.
As a junior officer he participated in the war with Mexico.
He knows the terrain there south of Texas, in particular
through Chihuahua, up through the mountains of Torreón,
and into the Central Valley to Zacatecas, San Luis Potosí,
and on to Mexico City.

"He served with dedication, if not brilliance. Seemed to
resent the authority of his superiors. After the Treaty of
Guadalupe Hidalgo, he ended his campaigning as a major.
After the war he was posted to various assignments in the
East and two frontier commands. He attended the War Col-
lege and was promoted to lieutenant colonel in fifty-five.
When the War Between the States broke out, he was promoted to colonel and given command of a regiment in Dal-
ton's brigade in the Army of the Potomac. Again, fate
seemed destined to withhold from him the glory achieved
by some, like Sherman and Custer. He was passed over
three times for brigadier and ended the war as he had begun
it. Since then he has been passed over a fourth time."

"All of which might make the man a wee bit bitter?"
O'Grady prompted.

"That is our considered opinion," the President answered
dryly. "Now, then, Mr. O'Grady, I want you to locate Kilgore and bring the man to justice. And, while you're at it,
to return to the jurisdiction of the United States Army any
and all of those in this with him," Johnson went on.

"How am I to go about this? What limits are placed on
me?"

"Let me send for coffee and some light lunch, then we'll
go into that," the President suggested.

Canyon O'Grady knew then that this would be a long and difficult day.

Giddily wavering sheets of heat-distorted air reduced visibility to less than a hundred yards. The trail had been long and hard since entering the vast emptiness of the Chihuahua desert. The only main road led to the capital city of Chihuahua, a population center far too large to be safe for the column of deserters Kilgore led. So far they had accomplished little.

On the second day in Mexico, the thirty-five freebooters had ridden into the small village of El Carrizo. Shooting into the air, yelling ferociously, the troopers had quickly cowed the hamlet. No one offered resistance. Kilgore appropriated three carts, high, solid-wheeled vehicles with tall, outward-sloping sides. Though the carts were usually pulled by a single ox, Kilgore ordered yokes and harness made to accommodate mules.

Then he directed the carts to be loaded with everything of value in El Carrizo. When the people protested, several men were shot. It took little time to collect the treasures of the poor community. Food, bags of water, liquor, and the precious objects from the church all went into the loot. Then, to the wailing of the women, Colonel Kilgore and his men rode off into the desert.

All of the food and water had long since been exhausted. Crossing from west to east in the bare land, they had failed to encounter a single oasis. Many of the men had emptied their canteens. Lance Means had exhausted his whiskey supply and suffered the torments of the damned for want of more.

He would be dried out soon, Colonel Kilgore considered. That would be a blessing. Sometime during the war, Lance Means had turned to the bottle for solace. Some said he had stayed drunk ever since. But drunk or sober, Lancelot Means was one of the finest tacticians Jud Kilgore had ever known. And he was a terror in combat no matter his condition. Kilgore recalled the billows of alcohol fumes emanating from the hard-faced captain at the crossing of the Rio Grande. Like himself, Lancelot Means had been passed over for promotion repeatedly. The severe cuts in the size of the army since the end of the war did not account for it alone. No, fate had slipped by them, judging both and finding them wanting.

" '*Mene, mene, tekel upharsin,*' " he quoted aloud. " 'You have been judged and found wanting.' "

"What's that?" Captain Means asked from his position to the left and a length behind Kilgore's horse.

"Uh—nothing, Lance, nothing at all. Damn, there has to be water here somewhere."

"You would think so," Means agreed. "Right now I'd sell my soul for a tin cup of cool, sweet water." Means blinked at his unbelievable statement and made a wry moue of his thick lips. "Did I say that? It only goes to show how dangerously far conditions have deteriorated."

"By God, Lance, you haven't used that good a vocabulary since you discovered old Waterfill-Frazier. Tell me, does it bother you, drying out?"

Means considered it a moment. "Truthfully, no, Jud. Not a great deal. Oh, I sometimes feel like there are ants crawling all over me, and my gut wants to crawl up and keep company with my Adam's apple. But I haven't been . . . so aware of things in a long time. Like . . . individual grains of sand. Of the touch of a soft breeze after this damned desert sun goes down." He chuckled deprecatingly. "I've even started hankering for a woman."

Smiling, Kilgore replied, "You can wet your wick to your heart's content once we get to the mountains. First there's loot to be taken."

"Is that where we're headed? The Sierra Madres?"

Kilgore's cold gray eyes narrowed. "Time enough to discuss that later. First we have to find water. Sergeant Gruber."

"Sir!" Gruber, who would have been wearing sergeant major's chervrons if he didn't have a tendency to be too brutal on young privates, gigged his horse forward.

"Inform the two scouts riding with us to move out ahead, I want them to leave the point men where they are and range farther. We have to find water."

"Right away, sir."

"One day, Sergeant. Have them take provisions for half a day out and half back."

"As you will, sir."

"They'll have to find water within that time," Means opined hopefully.

"They will or we won't be around to complain about it," Kilgore confided.

Government offices had begun to empty for the day when Canyon O'Grady walked out the gate of the White House onto Pennsylvania Avenue. A pair of deep furrows slashed his brow horizontally, with a companion upright between his coppery brows. His new assignment troubled him.

Kilgore and his renegades had either chosen to ride west, into the emptiness of Arizona perhaps, or headed south into Mexico. The President had impressed upon him the need for secrecy in carrying out the mission. Also discretion, tact, and, most of all, absolute success. What a hell of a lot to expect of one man alone. He couldn't even call upon military or civilian authorities to assist, until he had Kilgore in custody. And if he had to go into Mexico, he could not contact their officials at all. Why, he wondered, hadn't the President literally tied his hands behind him?

Shrugging it off, O'Grady whistled up a hansom cab—an enterprise that took five minutes and nine drivers who ignored him. He climbed into the tenth vehicle with dispatch.

"Union Station, driver."

"That's clear across town," the hackey complained.

"I'm sure you can find a fare at the depot," O'Grady affirmed.

With the rush of departing officeholders and the swarm of bureaucrats, it took fully twenty minutes to go from Lafayette Park to the impressive three-story railroad station on Virginia Avenue. The gray granite edifice, with huge seated stone lions guarding the brass-bound glass entranceway, impressed O'Grady in spite of his intimate knowledge of the awesome Rocky Mountains. He passed through the story-high portals onto polished pink Carrara marble floors. He went immediately from the crush of the homeward-bound to that of distant travelers.

Long lines extended from each of the open ticket windows. O'Grady took his place in the proper one and settled in to wait. Much of the government agent's disdain for "civilization" had do with the crowding. For all the open space and free land to the west, more than three-quarters of the population remained east of the Atlantic Range—the Catskill, Allegheny, Blue Ridge, and Cumberland mountains.

He preferred the empty frontier to the constant press of bodies.

It bred poverty, violence, and corruption. Politicians became more important than parents. Large numbers of people required large numbers of police. The opportunities for abuse of the system increased proportionately. But not in the open, free air of the frontier. There men tended their own business, spoke their minds freely, and fought to defend what they had when necessary. Small wonder that the longest line in the Washington railroad station was at the window for travel beyond the Ohio River.

Before his father had sent him to Ireland to continue his education, Canyon O'Grady had known only the confines of urban life. Even as a child he had chaffed under its repressive atmosphere. As an adult, he found even less to recommend it.

"Where to?"

Blinking away his reverie, O'Grady found himself at the head of the line. Beyond the wrought-iron grille in the dark wood of the ticket counter, an entirely bald man, his face concealed in part by a green eyeshade, glowered at him as though resentful of anyone with the ability to escape the blessings of "civilization."

"Texas. San Antonio or as far west of there as I can go."

"Well, now," the ticket agent muttered as he flipped through the pages of a schedule catalog. "You can take the Short Line to Richmond, lay over a day, then the Dixie to Atlanta. Day and a half there, then the Cotton Belt to New Orleans. Nine hours' layover there, then take the Texas and Pacific to San Antonio and on as far as Eagle Pass. Total travel time, seven and a half days. Or . . ." he added quickly, tongue-wetted thumb busy in the pages again, "you can take the B and O to Cleveland, overnight stay there, then the Illinois Central to St. Louis. Three-hour layover to take the Katy—the Missouri, Kansas, and Texas—from St. Louis to San Antonio, and be in Eagle Pass the next day, for a total of four and a half days."

"I'll take it. The second one," O'Grady told him.

"First, second, or third class? With first class you have the Hotel Express, with sleeping accommodations in a Pullman parlor car, and take your meals in the dining car. Second class is chair car, you catch your meals on the run at sched-uled stops, and third is bench seating, no heat in the cars, and you better buy off the candy butcher or risk losing your place."

O'Grady thought less than a second. After all, the special fund for the President's agents was paying his expenses. "First class. And I need accommodations for my horse. He's in St. Louis at present and will have to be boarded there."

"Fine, fine. That'll be a hundred dollars, plus four dollars a day for meals, through to San Antonio, and forty dollars for stock-car space for the horse. That's if you take care of it yourself. Two dollars a day for the crew to feed and water the animal."

Cormac, O'Grady's palomino stallion, didn't take well to strangers. O'Grady considered it prudent, then, for him to see to the horse's care. "I'll tend to my horse, thank you," he answered. From one pocket he fetched out one hundred and forty dollars in twenty-dollar gold pieces, and sixteen more in coin and paper currency.

Like the head and neck of a snapping turtle, the pale, bony hand and arm of the ticket clerk darted out and drew in the money, which he counted critically. Then he set about making up the ticket, lettering in brown ink and blotting entries of train numbers, times, and accommodations. When he completed these, he decorated each slip with multiple strikes of rubber stamps in a variety of colors.

These were placed together in an arcane pattern known only to the railway agent, and punctured with a spring-loaded hole punch. A cover was provided and the lot stapled together. This he shoved into an envelope, which he handed to O'Grady.

"The Short Line Number 401 departs here tomorrow morning, seven-forty. Don't be late."

Outside Union Station he cornered a cab and rode to the Daniel Webster. In his suite, he found the situation apparently unchanged from when he departed. The only exception was that fresh hot water had been provided for the tub. Eyebrows rising, he took it all in.

"It appears you have thought of everything, my dear. You are truly lovely, Moira my lass, and I'm eager to join you in the festivities you have planned. But first, love, I have a sad duty to perform. I must pack, at once."

Moira put small fists on her satisfyingly flared bare hips. "What do you mean, 'pack'?"

"My clothes. That business I went to tend to. It makes it necessary that I leave first thing in the morning."

"But that's so . . . so soon. I had plans for us. Dinner, a long night of pleasure, tomorrow a picnic in the Virginia woods."

"It will all have to wait for another visit to Washington, I'm afraid." From the closet he withdrew his army-style wooden footlocker and opened it.

He folded and put away the spare suit of clothes hanging there, then turned to the dresser. From it he took shirts and underclothing and put them in the lower portion of the trunk. Grumbling, Moira retrieved a scuffed and well-used pair of boots from the armoire and wrapped them in a towel. These she laid in with the rest. At last everything O'Grady had brought with him from St. Louis had been packed. Moira looked into his face, fire in her eyes.

"Is that all?"

"No. I have to get the hotel boy to come up and have my suit pressed."

Moira stamped her foot. "Canyon O'Grady, are you dense? Here I stand, naked as the day God made me, and you talk about getting your suit pressed. Haven't you any feelings? Aren't you even a little fussed and bothered?"

Tie first, then the shirt came off. O'Grady took a step toward the beguiling nude who ornamented his suite. "I am more than a little fussed," he allowed in a bantering tone. "And I am most definitely bothered."

"What is bothering you?"

"I can't . . . seem to get . . . this belt buckle undone," O'Grady answered through a chuckle. "Or my trousers off quickly enough."

"Why would you want to do that?" Moira retorted, joining the game.

"Because that is the only way I can make wild, unstinting love to you until your eyes cross and your breath comes in short pants."

Moira made a face of wide-eyed innocence. "Oh, dear, I thought only naughty little boys came in their short pants."

O'Grady grimaced. He hated puns, even risqué ones. "If these pesky buttons will only cooperate, I'll give you something better to play with than words."

"Oh? Oh, yes. I think I vaguely recall something that came up in the tub. Is that right?"

Then he stood before her, totally unclothed and fully aroused. Moira uttered a squeal of joy and rushed to his arms. Their lips met openmouthed and his tongue flashed boldly into the waiting cavern. Moira ground the stygian thatch of her pubic mound into the hardness of his up-curved member. With one hand O'Grady held the back of her head. The other strayed down the symmetrical curve of her back to her firm round buttocks.

O'Grady tweaked a firm breast, the nipple of which had been boring into his chest as it hardened in ardor, then lifted Moira and carried her through the door to the waiting bed. He placed her gently and crawled between widespread legs. His hands quickly attentive to her needs, he manipu-lated Moira to new heights of arousal.

"Oh, Canyon, Canyon, oh my. Ooooh!" Moira keened.

Then he took her, smoothly, swiftly, to the hilt. Her eyes flew open and her mouth twisted in a grimace of pure plea-sure. Supported on his elbows, he made long, sliding strokes that sent shivers of delight through both of them. Euphoria awaited far down the line, something to be anticipated and forestalled for deliciously stimulating decades of minutes.

Moira peaked after a seemingly endless time and O'Grady continued to rock in the primal rhythm. The con-fining walls faded and a galaxy of stars filled an ebon, velvet night. Two souls sought to meld into a single entity, one consumed by ecstasy.

"Oh, damn," the constantly vigilant corner of O'Grady's mind prodded him. If it kept on being this good, he might miss his train.

3

Another four or five hours and it would be all over with. Colonel Judson Kilgore looked back at the drooping ranks of his soldiers and admitted the terrible truth to himself. For the past hour, though it was hardly past midmorning, they had been compelled to walk, leading their mounts. Three horses had died regardless of that. The troopers' personal gear, saddles, and accoutrements had been distributed among their comrades. Worse, the draft animals had suffered mightily.

All items of low value had been thrown off the carts the previous day. The teamsters led the wagons now, instead of adding their weight to the burdens. Mules might have greater stamina than horses, Kilgore reasoned, but under the conditions dictated by this desert, nothing short of reptiles and insects would survive for long without water. Where were the scouts he had sent out in search of water?

In violation of his own order, Judson Kilgore swung into the saddle and forced his flagging mount into a dispirited shuffle that approximated a trot. Ahead the horizon had been blotted out by a rising swale in the blighted terrain. The shimmering heat waves and sheer size of the cordillera proved deceiving.

Kilgore didn't reach the crest until nearly twenty minutes had elapsed. Panting in the heat, mouth parchment dry and aching, he hadn't the strength to dismount. Red-rimmed eyes that felt constantly abraded by fine grains of windblown sand watered as he tried to look forward. Suddenly he stiffened. His oft-deceived senses tried to reject what he thought he saw.

Far off, distorted by the waterfall effect of rising thermal shafts, a brown smudge could be seen intermittently near the horizon. It could be a dust storm building, Colonel Kilgore thought in a moment of panic. Or it could be the scouts returning. They had taken along a packhorse and four water tuns. Could it be them? Could they be coming back with good news and life-saving water? Then again, it might be the Mexican Army.

No, it had to be the scouts. Shakily Kilgore pulled his field glasses from their leather case. The brass eyepieces burned against his skin when he put them to his face. His long, spatulate index finger fumbled with the focus knob. Murkily the distance resolved itself. Then the scene snapped into startling clarity.

Triple plumes of dust, churned up by pounding hooves, merged into one large billow that strung out behind two riders and an animal on a lead. Lumpy shapes under a tarpaulin on the packhorse's back resolved into the water casks. New hope leapt in Kilgore's heart. They'd made it. They had come back with water. Eagerly he continued to advance ahead of the column.

In twenty minutes he could see the features of the scouts. They looked rested and undaunted by the enormous heat. Judson Kilgore imagined he could see mist, a smoky vapor, rising from the barrels. Another ten minutes and the scouts rumbled to a halt before him. Both saluted smartly and Corporal Dahlinger made his report.

"We found it, sir. Plenty of water. There's a town—Juimes, it's called. Nice little place. We didn't locate anything yesterday, so we rested awhile and kept going. Around ten o'clock we saw lights, heard music. There's a river there, sir. Not much of one, but it's running, clean and sweet. We refreshed, got a meal, and filled our barrels."

"We also found out there's a bigger town, Saucillo, a day's ride south of Juimes," the second scout added.

"Good. Excellent, men. I shall prepare proper commendation later. Now, get that back to the troops and issue it out to men and animals. And, ah, after he's had a drink and tended his horse, send Captain Means forward to me."

"As you wish, sir," the corporal returned. "And yourself, sir? What about water for the colonel, sir?"

"Ju-just let me fill my canteen and I'll be all right."

Twenty minutes later Lancelot Means joined the renegade colonel. "It sounds too good to be true. We made it all the way across this cursed desert and didn't lose a man. Only three or four hours' ride to Juimes?"

"That's what Dahlinger said. They left before daybreak this morning to get water to us. It's not enough, but it will do until we get to Juimes."

"I'm relieved. You know, there's something I've been considering. We ought to dispose of these uniforms at the earliest convenience."

"I don't see why," Kilgore answered testily.

"American uniforms are hardly a guarantee of hospitable treatment by the locals, Jud. Further, if the Mexican government takes it in mind we are here officially, they might open hostilities with the United States."

"Nothing I'd like better. With them busy fighting a new war, there won't be time for them to pay us much mind."

Means tilted his head to one side, signifying his doubt. "More likely, they'll swarm down to wipe us out, being the closest example of Yanqui imperialism they can put a hand on.''

"Won't make any difference anyway. Once we get all the water we want and rest up in Juimes, we advance on Saucillo. Everything will be going our way.''

"How's that?''

"When we've all recovered, we're going to strip that town of everything of value and not leave any witnesses. We'll kill every man, woman, and child.''

"By God, you sound like your old self now, Jud. Remember in that Comanch' village? 'Don't mind the warriors, boys. Kill the women and kids, burn everything to the ground.' ''

"For which I earned an official reprimand, you recall,'' Colonel Kilgore stated with flat bitterness. "I don't understand it, Sheridan, Sherman, Custer, Carrington all think the same way, say so out loud to the journalists. They don't get passed over for promotion, they don't get assigned to the asshole of creation, they don't get called 'Barbarians in Blue.' Ugh! Whoever came up with that epithet ought to be taken out and shot. Anyway, they're busy openly planning the extermination of the red man, and not a word of criticism. All I do is lift a little squaw hair and the mushheads back East, the sob-story writers, all want to crucify me.'' He drew a deep breath, gathered his grievances under control.

"Well, by God, I'll tell you this,'' Kilgore went on in a milder tone. "What we do in Juimes and Saucillo will be a message for them all. Mark my words, they'll learn how it ought to be done.''

Under a broiling post-noon sun, Canyon O'Grady eased himself in the saddle and wiped dust from his sweaty face. From his vantage point among a jumble of mustard-yellow and muddy-brown boulders atop a long high ridge, he looked down at the town of Eagle Pass, Texas. At this distance the buildings looked like scattered blocks thrown down by a giant's playful child.

Smoke rose from a tall tin stovepipe at one narrow end of a large rectangle. Its sides unpainted and weathered an unhealthy gray, it had the pallor of death. Small dots, which had to be children, made irregular patterns of random movement in the schoolyard. A wide, much-traveled road bisected the community to the north and south of it. Another thoroughfare pointed due south from one side of the main street at an expanded intersection, its terminus a bridge that spanned the Rio Grande to Piedras Negras, Coahuila, Mexico.

At this hub of commerce, a windmill towered over a large wooden water trough, its blades turning lazily in a light South Texas breeze. An octagonal bandstand occupied this intersection also, and from its elevated position, O'Grady judged that the equipment of the volunteer fire department was housed below the floorboards of the band platform. He could see the same thing from Ohio to Kansas, Nebraska to New Orleans. Even the frontier was becoming predictable.

O'Grady pushed back his hat brim, exposing the prominent widow's peak of ruddy hair. There had been a telegram waiting for him in San Antonio. It came not from Alan Pinkerton, head of the recently created Secret Service, but from Major General Joshua Colton, aide to the President for Special Services, O'Grady's boss. It informed him that three officers, including Captain Lancelot Means and Second Lieutenant Edward Kilgore, six noncommissioned officers, including Sergeant Howard Gruber, and twenty-five enlisted men had deserted with Colonel Judson Kilgore. It also stated that witnesses had verified that the renegades had turned south and apparently entered the state of Chihuahua, Mexico. And concluded with a reminder that time was of the essence.

Hell of a deal, O'Grady considered. He had been directed to enter Mexico covertly and effect the removal of Kilgore and as many of his men as possible without alarming the Mexican authorities. Well, he had pulled off the near-impossible before. Perhaps he shouldn't have been so efficient. To add to his difficulties, an article in the San Antonio *Gazette* blew to shreds the cloak of secrecy the President wanted on the whole affair.

It related the sacking of El Carrizo, in Chihuahua, by an outlaw band described as "army deserters and outlaws from north of the border." Survivors of the attack indicated that the marauders had headed southeast from El Carrizo. So, instead of heading west from Eagle Pass, he would go south. To add insult to the harm already done, that morning the Texas and Pacific *Daylight Flier* had had a minor breakdown at a whistle stop twenty miles east of Eagle Pass.

Rather than wait a night and a day while replacement parts were "rushed" from San Antonio, O'Grady had cajoled the train crew into dropping the ramp door on the stock car and releasing Cormac, his palomino stallion named for an eighth-century Irish king. He could easily ride the distance to Eagle Pass in less than four hours. He would lay over until his baggage arrived.

Hopefully Eagle Pass would have accommodations better than the haymow in a livery stable where he could put his head down for a good night's rest. It might be his last for a long time. Accepting his fate—after all, it came with the job—Canyon O'Grady gigged Cormac with blunted spurs and twitched the reins. Slowly, snorting at the scent of water from the Rio Grande, the big palomino began to thread its way through the rocks.

Saucillo had not been easy. Colonel Judson Kilgore had to admit he had underestimated the ability and willingness of the Mexican people to resist the depredations of his wandering band of brigands. The Ejército de República—the Mexican Army—had an infantry section in Saucillo. By example and patient guidance, the soldiers had led the populace in bloody clashes in the streets of the town.

Unlike El Carrizo and Juimes, Kilgore lost three men and had seven wounded before the defenders had been routed. The fighting had begun the moment a shopkeeper spotted the blue uniforms of his troop. Once more Lancelot Means's tactical savvy had proved accurate. More than that, his understanding of the strategic requirements for future success outweighed the benefit of uniforms helping enforce discipline. Before leaving Saucillo, his men divested themselves of enough army clothing and equipment to not look "military."

That had been four days in the past. It had served well during their crossover into Coahuila. With less than a day's ride to Ciudad Malchor, Kilgore once more felt a soaring confidence. He remained unruffled even when a point rider galloped back with electrifying news.

"Riders beyond that ridge, sir. Soldiers, sir. It's the Mexican Army."

"What's their strength?" Colonel Kilgore asked calmly.

"They're ridin' four abreast, about ten ranks deep, sir.

Two sections. With the officers and supply train, I'd say maybe ninety-five strong."

"How long before they reach this point?" came the colonel's next question.

The advance man considered it. "They're walkin' now, sir. Unless they go to a gallop next, say . . . fifteen, twenty minutes."

"Halt the troop, Lance," Kilgore commanded Means. "We'll want them dug in to either side of the road. Along . . . there and there." His eyes searched their surroundings. "Set some men to chopping down some of those big cacti. They're to use their horses to drag them onto the road and form a blockade. Have Sergeant Nally bring up that pack-horse with the blasting powder."

"Right away, sir," Means responded, the eager hunger for battle glowing in his light brown eyes. "Troo-op . . . Halt!"

Captain Means quickly explained the situation to the sergeants, adding details from past experience, who set about barking orders at the men. Small pack shovels made the sandy soil fly. When Sergeant Nally reported to the colonel, he was given a special task. He would convert sticks of blasting powder, caps, and fuse into buried mines that would turn the roadway into a treacherous trap. The sergeant called for five men to help him.

Fifteen minutes fled like the blink of an eye. So far no Mexican troops had topped the rise. Through the bawling NCOs, Kilgore urged more haste. He inspected the hastily dug firing pits of the soldiers and made an occasional suggestion for improvement. Another five minutes went into history.

"Where are they?" Lance Means demanded, impatient to get into the fighting.

"Not too far, I would judge," Kilgore retorted.

Their point had been pulled back in order not to alert the Mexican soldiers. One man crouched in a wind-sculptured rock formation on the skyline created by the ridge. He would signal when the Mexicans came within half a mile. And again when they neared the top of the rise. From then on, surprise offered the principal tactic upon which Colonel Kilgore could rely.

"It's Gordon, sir," Means spoke eagerly. "That's the signal."

"Good. Then it's time you and I got out of sight. You men at the roadblock," he went on, raising his voice, "stand by. They're coming."

Less than five minutes later the second signal came from Private Gordon. Tiny pinpricks of light appeared first. Then a forest of slender poles supporting them. Lances, borne by men whose crested and plumed helmets came into view next. Kilgore's eyes widened at the sight. He had heard of the prowess of the Mexican lancers; now he would find out how good they really were. Damn, if he had only salvaged Camp Fenton's solitary six-pounder. A little artillery would do well.

Broad shoulders in splendid green-and-white uniforms emerged over the top of the ridge, along with tossing horses' heads. The vangard crested the rise. From his position to command the field, Colonel Kilgore studied the enemy leader through his field glasses. He saw the rigid, militarily correct features dissolve into an expression of surprise. The Mexican commander raised his hand to signal a halt as his face reformed into resolute anticipation.

"Los bandidos norteños," the Mexican colonel said with satisfaction, his tone low and purring. *"¡Alinear en forma de asalto!"* Instantly obedient to the command, the lancers moved into line abreast, three ranks deep.

"¡Lanzas al punto!" Down came the highly polished nickel-plate tips of the deadly spears.

"¡Tocar la embestida!" Shrill and brazen, the notes of the "Charge" rippled from the trumpeter's horn.

Extending his hand over his head, the colonel swung it downward smartly. *"¡Ataque! ¡Ataque!"*

With shrill whinnies, the perfectly matched grays lunged forward and thundered down the slope toward the improvised roadblock. In a space of thirty yards they reached a full gallop. Clouds of dark red-brown dust boiled up from their hooves. The trumpeter continued to blow the staccato summons to battle. An animal roar of anticipatory bloodlust came from the throats of the *lanzeros.*

"Didn' waste no goddamn time, did they?" Sergeant Nally observed dryly to Colonel Kilgore. "When you want me to light these fuses?"

"Wait until they are fully engaged at the roadblock."

On they came, their lusty *huzzahs!* shivering the air.

Lance points in perfect alignment, they appeared a formidable, nay an invincible, juggernaut that sped downhill toward the fragile barricade of saguaro cacti that had been piled across the road and off to the sides. These formed the closed end of a long box, the sides of which were seasoned riflemen who enjoyed the art of killing. In the tense moment before the lancers closed on the blockade, Colonel Kilgore raised his voice in sharp command.

"Left and right echelon . . . by the volley . . . Fire! . . . Fire! . . . *Fire!*"

The thunderous roar of discharging rifles drowned out his commands. Horses reared and shrilled in pain and dismay. Riders fell from the saddles, lances went clattering to the ground. The second file crashed on the ruin of the first, waded through, and engaged the few men at the barricade. The third file closed in.

"Fuses now, if you please, Sergeant," Kilgore coolly commanded.

Short powder trains sputtered and burned briefly. Suddenly the writhing panoply of battle washed bright white and all motion froze for an instant. Earth-shattering noise followed, in company with the fading of the blast through yellow to orange and red. Dust and black smoke melded with cottony puffs of powder fume to form a dense pall over the point of conflict. Bits and pieces of riding tack, uniforms, horse and human flesh whizzed through the choked air.

When the tumult ended, fewer than thirty lancers remained upright. A dozen of these had raised their hands in surrender. Before the fatal blows could be struck, one of them called out shrilly to the victors.

"Do not shoot! We want to join you. You are truly great warriors. Do not shoot us."

Swiftly the other, loyal troops were cut down. Colonel Kilgore looked on in bemused speculation. He had gained a victory over a far superior force, and much more. He now had a dozen trained, capable fighting men to replace the eight men of his own who had so far been sacrificed in battle. He licked dry lips and considered this with elation. His prospects soared!

4

School had ended for the day by the time Canyon O'Grady reached the outskirts of Eagle Pass. Barefoot and noisy, a band of boys, their school shoes tied by the laces around their necks, ran around and past him, intent on some youthful adventure of which they alone knew. He ambled on to the railroad depot.

There he inquired about his baggage, to learn that the train would not be in until the next day. Temporarily thwarted, O'Grady located the town's only hotel, the Lone Star Rest. For fifty cents he engaged a room for the night. An additional half-dollar ensured he had one "by himself."

Satisfied with the accommodations, he took Cormac to the livery to have him stabled, rubbed down, and given a double ration of grain that night and in the morning. Saddlebags over one shoulder, he walked back toward the hotel. He kept alert for some sign of a suitable place to take his evening meal. True to his expectation, he found none. He did mark one greasy-plate operation as a possibility a moment before the headline on a newspaper caught his eye: "MEXICO ACCUSES TEXICANS OF RAIDING ACROSS BORDER."

Bold black letters spelled out the accusation. O'Grady whistled to the small lad hawking the local rag on a corner. The tousle-haired youngster skipped up to him, long hanks of dusty light-brown hair bouncing with each jerky stride.

"That'll be a nickel, mister."

O'Grady fished a coin from his pocket. "Here you go, boy." He spread the front page of the *Lone Star Clarion* and read the subhead aloud: " 'Bandits Sack Chihuahua, Coahuila.' "

In the first paragraph the bandits were described as "American outlaws, including army deserters, who raided and looted the towns of El Carrizo, Juimes, and Saucillo in Chihuahua, and Santa Clara in Coahuila." It described the viciousness of these attacks and pointed out few survivors remained in any of the victimized towns.

Witnesses in differing locations pointed out that the English-speaking bandits referred to their leader as Colonel, so Mexican journalists and some government spokesmen had labled him Coronel Muerte—Colonel Death. O'Grady could glean little else of useful intelligence from the florid prose of the author. He knew one thing, though, that apparently none of these others did. He had no doubt as to the identity of Colonel Death.

In the Ciudad Malchor, Coahuila, cantina Bajo el Cielo de México—Under Mexican Skies—five Americans sat at a table along the wall opposite the bar. They drank and talked quietly among themselves. Across from them, high boot heels hooked over the brass rail, stood three locals, all dressed alike.

They wore tight-legged rust-brown trousers, half-dollar-size conchos along the outer leg seams, fancy-front white shirts, short-cut jackets, and matching neck scarves served as foulard ties. Each had belted to his narrow hips a brace of revolvers, with crossed bandoliers of preloaded paper cartridges in leather tubes that resembled cigar cases over their chests. They drank in a sullen silence and glanced frequently at the Americans.

"I have a feeling those fellows don't take a liking to us," Lieutenant Edward Kilgore remarked in a low tone.

"Rough-looking lot," Captain Lance Means added. "Could be *pistoleros*—gunmen."

"Or they might be the local law," Colonel Judson Kilgore suggested. "The Rurales. Whoever they are, we'd best keep an eye on them."

"Won't matter for long," Edward Kilgore opined. "The boys'll be in position anytime now, and then it'll all be over."

At the far end of the saloon, against the narrow back wall, a musician in similar costume to the trio, although in black, picked up his guitar and strummed a few chords. The violinist next to him bowed his instrument and twisted pegs to change key. The trumpeter let go a riff of golden notes. Another, fatter, guitar joined in. After exchanging a few quiet words with his companions, the hatchet-faced gunman at the bar stepped out a pace and called to the mariachis.

"¡Oye! Tocarle el Degüello."

Exchanging nervous glances, the mariachis looked at the Americans. Each hesitated to strike up the opening bar. An expression of disgust twisted the hatchet-faced caballero. He dug into one pocket and came out with a handful of peso coins. These he hurled in the direction of the musicians.

"Andale pues," he growled. *"Tocarle, tocarle."*

In breathy syncopation the guitars began the introduction. The violin joined in. Stinging in, the trumpet took up the theme. The ghostly, haunting notes filled the saloon.

"Jeezus, what's that?" Edward Kilgore asked. "It makes the hairs rise on the back of my neck."

"I don't know," Lance Means answered. "I don't often pay attention to someone when he requests a song."

"That's because you're tone deaf as a post," Judson Kilgore responded. "You have better Spanish than me, Lance. What's . . . ah . . . *'degüello'* mean?"

For all his experiences and courage in battle, Lance Means blanched. "Throat-cutting. It's supposed to be what the Mexicans played for those boys in the Alamo."

At the bar, the sharp-featured man locked his gaze on that of Colonel Kilgore. He worked his mouth in an insolent manner and spat on the floor. Then he squared off with the American and licked the web of his left hand. He reached behind him without looking and curled his fingers around a shooter of tequila. One companion deposited a pinch of salt on the web and balanced a slice of lime on the glass.

Not breaking his fixed stare, the local tough brought the liquor around to his face. White teeth split his face as he licked the salt, then bit into the lime. This he also spat in the direction of the Americans before he downed the tequila in a single gulp. At once he began an angry tirade.

"Gringo cabrones. Asesinos de las mujeres y niños. Corrómperos de la puerza de Mexico."

"Yankee assholes," Lance Means translated in *sotto voce*. "Murderers of women and children. Corrupters of the purity of Mexico."

"Don't take kindly to us, does he?" Edward Kilgore forced a jest, though his muddled blue-gray eyes registered the fear that gripped him.

Not satisfied with the lack of effect of his words, the

pistolero began to stride toward their table, his right hand on the use-worn butt of an old Mendoza copy of the Colt Dragoon. The five Americans remained motionless, Colonel Kilgore with his hands resting in his lap, out of sight under the table. The insults grew more caustic.

"*¡Pendejos, ladrones, bastardos! Querenos chingada sus madres. Mierdo en la leche de sus madres,*" he snarled with increasing menace.

"Panderers, thieves, bastards," Lance faithfully translated. "We will fuck your mothers. I shit in the milk of your mothers."

By that point, the enraged gunman stepped to a place some four feet from their table. Suddenly wood erupted from the surface, followed by a lance of flame and smoke behind the bullet fired by Judson Kilgore. It struck their detractor in the throat. He staggered backward a pace and toppled to one side onto the floor.

"That's done it! Let's get 'em!" Captain Lance Means shouted.

At once gunfire erupted throughout the cantina. Lance Means accounted for one of the dead man's companions. The other pistolero got off a shot before Sergeant Gruber put a ball in his chest. He went to his knees in front of the bar, one hand groping at the hole that seeped blood. A second bullet smashed into his brain while he tried feebly to lift his heavy revolver.

While the fancily dressed gunmen died, Edward Kilgore expended several rounds destroying bottles and glasses behind the bar before he plunked a .44-caliber ball into the *cantinero*. The barman sagged, clutching at his shoulder, and reached for a short-barreled shotgun under the counter. When he came up with it, he caught another ball between his eyes, fired by Lieutenant Rupert Dibble.

Shouting wildly at this scene of demented bloodshed, the musicians sought safety in flight. They became the next to die. In less than three minutes, only the five outlaw soldiers remained alive in the saloon. Quickly they went about stripping the corpses of all money, arms, and ammunition. Captain Means emptied the till and added the cantina's income to the take. Satisfied, Colonel Kilgore started for the door.

"Make a thorough job of it," he commanded. "I'll be outside."

On the street he could clearly hear the discharge of many

weapons as his troops went about their mission of subduing the populace and looting every business. To his left he heard a shrill scream and turned in time to see a shapely young woman dart out the side door of a dress shop.

She wore an attractive multicolored skirt which she hiked high to facilitate running. Behind her came two men in remnants of uniform. Grinning lewdly, they chased after her. Eyes wide with fright, mouth twisted into a grimace of desperation and horror, she came abreast of Colonel Kilgore, who wore the costume of a well-to-do Mexican gentleman.

"*¡Socorro! Señor. ¡Socorro! Por amor de Dios, ayudame,*" she wailed her appeal.

There was no help for her this day, from God or anyone else. Her pursuers caught up to her in two more strides. Each seized an arm and lifted her off her feet. Her legs still flailing the air, they carried her to the mouth of a nearby alley. Moments later, the sound of her screams and the tearing of cloth reached Colonel Kilgore's ears. An angry scowl formed below his thick shock of gray-shot ebon hair. With quick strides he walked to the alley.

One soldier stood over the girl, who had been pinned to the ground by his companion. He fumbled with his fly as Kilgore entered the narrow passage. "Enough of that," the colonel thundered.

Both men looked at their commander in disbelief. Raging inside, Colonel Kilgore gave vent to the cause of his anger. "There are a hell of a lot more places to loot, wagons to load. Save that for afterward. Now, get back to your assigned duties or I'll have you flogged."

"Sir, yes, sir!" they shouted, leaping away from the supine girl. Their lips curled in sullen pouts, they headed back to the plundering.

Long, slanting lines of purple, rose, tangerine, and gray streaked the western sky when O'Grady departed for the hash house he had decided upon for supper. One whiff of the interior and he concluded he could do better with a beer and the free lunch at a saloon. Faint music tinkled from a piano in one relatively uncrowded establishment, so O'Grady pushed through the batwings and advanced on the bar.

Close to the marble-topped mahogany-paneled counter he noticed several marked differences from the usual frontier saloon. For one, he became aware of muslin sheeting that hung in cloud-belly billows from the ceiling. Also, he didn't see any spittoons. Instead, a long square-sided tile trough ran the length of the bar. Water sluiced along it suddenly as he came nearer. Puzzled, he wondered at its purpose until he caught a slight scent of stale urine. No. It couldn't be used for that.

"What'll you have?" the barman asked in a friendly rumble.

"Beer," O'Grady said, eyes on the accumulation at the near end of the mahogany.

"You want a glass, schooner, bucket, or bottle?"

Surprised, O'Grady paused a moment. "Schooner. I didn't expect such a choice this far from any brewery."

"Oh, we got our own brewery. Lone Star Beer," the apron answered cheerfully.

What else? O'Grady rolled his eyes toward his hat brim. He kept a straight face, though, as the barkeep continued.

"Right good, too. Got as much flavor and body as Pabst or Anheiser's out of St. Loo."

"Bring it on," O'Grady urged. While the bartender drew the beer, he went to the free-lunch layout.

He found a choice of three types of bread, also tortillas, cold roast beef, sliced tongue, cold fried chicken, and pig's feet in vinegar jelly. A heavy duty glazed Mexican clay bowl held potato salad, another whole dill pickles in brine, a third hard-boiled eggs. Another pair held beans in chili gravy and cheese melted with beer and onions, kept hot over an apparatus with a layer of glowing charcoal. A tray of the same pottery material held a mound of triangular crisp tortilla chips.

Apparently the establishments in Eagle Pass catered to custom from both sides of the border, O'Grady decided. The flame-haired government agent helped himself to a sandwich of tongue, some chicken and pig's feet, potato salad, and a pair of eggs. In the space left on the oval platter provided for customer use, he dropped a handful of chips, covered them with beans and cheese.

"There's some chile peppers, if you've got the mouth and stomach for 'em," the bartender announced as he set down O'Grady's beer.

"I—ah—think I'll pass." He'd get enough of those for some time to come, O'Grady reckoned.

O'Grady munched contentedly for a while. Then his natural curiosity bump, that attribute that made him an excellent investigator and troubleshooter for the President, vibrated annoyingly. The bartender came by to refill his large thick beer schooner and O'Grady took the occasion to glance meaningfully toward the ceiling.

"What's the fancy decorations for?" he asked.

"Oh, that. To keep the scorpions and water bugs off our customers' necks. This desert country's full of bugs."

"Umm," O'Grady responded around a bite of hard-boiled egg. "And the trough down here?"

"That's to accommodate our customers from over the border. They're a two-fisted drinking lot and don't like to interrupt the serious business of getting *borracho* to go way out back to the chicksale."

"Downright considerate," O'Grady managed, dubious of the sanitation standards that implied. Forcing himself to ignore it, he worked away at the rest of his meal.

Darkness had wrapped Eagle Pass in a cloak of silence everywhere but on the bustling main street that led to Piedras Negras, when O'Grady exited from the Alamo Saloon. Constant traffic flowed both directions across the bridge. The dance halls and saloons of Eagle Pass gave off yellow washes of light and splashes of piano and fiddle music. In the distance, O'Grady could hear the lively twang and brassy blares of mariachi music from the cantinas of Piedras Negras. The local citizens seemed one big happy family, intent on pleasure, without regard to national borders.

That peaceful illusion lasted for the first block on his walk back to the hotel. O'Grady had reached the shadowed overhang of a general mercantile store on the corner when a voice arrested his movement and sent him into a tense crouch.

"I know you're there. Come on out. You've got one minute, Ballard."

Assured not to be the target of the challenge, O'Grady relaxed as a muffled reply came from a saloon half a block ahead. "Who's runnin' his mouth out there?"

"Texas Ranger, Ballard. Time's runnin' short. Come out of there with your hands in plain sight."

"The hell with that. Ain't nobody gonna take me back to hang. Come get me, Ranger."

Not his fight, O'Grady eased back into the shadows to

avoid the line of fire. It would also prevent any misunderstanding on the part of the lawman. Footsteps from behind crunched gravel near the center of the street. Sudden movement ahead changed O'Grady's mind.

Indistinct figures, darker blobs against blackness, appeared in the alleyway beside the saloon from which Ballard had issued his defiance. Another skulking silhouette materialized on the balcony overlooking the street. The Ranger came in line with O'Grady, and the President's agent spoke in a low, relaxed whisper.

"Easy, Ranger, I'm on your side."

"Oh, really?"

"You can take odds on it. Seems your boy Ballard has some friends along. There's two or more in the alley this side of that saloon, and another on the balcony behind that signboard."

"That figures. Still, it's my fight, Mr. . . . ?"

"Patrick. Michael Patrick." He used his given names—the ones Father Reardon had insisted upon in the face of his mother's preference for "Canyon"—to register at the hotel, and did so now.

"A mick, huh?" the Ranger responded. "You've got a gun on, can you use it?"

"I can hold my own," O'Grady answered with an invisible shrug.

"So, what do you intend to do with it?"

"Nothing, if Ballard gives himself up without a fight. If those boys jump you, I'll shoot them off your back."

"Let's hope they don't get that close. I catch your meaning, though. Obliged to have you take a hand. We'd best go now."

"I'll stay here. We'll keep it a surprise you've got company."

Quick footsteps carried the Ranger to the front of the saloon. Hand on the butt of his age-worn Walker Model 3 Colt, he paused and called out again. Immediately a bull of a man filled the open doorway. He already had a revolver in his hand, a slender-barreled Remington that spat fire at once.

His ball smacked meat in the Ranger's left shoulder, staggering him. He already had his weapon free of leather. Suddenly the upper front of the saloon washed white in the muzzle flash of the hidden assassin's six-gun. His round missed as the Ranger went to one knee. O'Grady didn't miss.

A hot round caught the would-be killer below his right armpit and ripped through both lungs. The hollow-base conical bullet O'Grady preferred to the standard .44 round ball deflected off the inside of the gunman's rib cage and plowed downward. Reflex drove him up and backward, blood gouting from his mouth and nose. At once the backup men in the alley reacted.

"What the hell?" one blurted, swinging toward the sound of the unexpected shot. Peering uncertainly, he raised the rifle he held to his shoulder.

O'Grady shot him in the gut. He did a pratfall and sat staring stupidly at the black hole in the spreading circle of numbness radiating from his abdomen. In the street, the Ranger fired again, splintering bone in Ballard's shoulder.

The outlaw squealed like a pig and cringed against the front of the saloon. His other protector, uncertain of where the shot had come from that felled his friend, stepped out into the street and took aim at the Ranger. O'Grady cocked his Model '60 Colt, the hammer notches clicking loudly in the momentary silence.

"Don't," O'Grady said simply.

Only a moment's hesitation passed before the back-shooter eased his rifle to the ground and threw up his hands. Coming to his feet, the Ranger advanced on his quarry and roughly fastened iron manacles to Ballard's wrists, bending them behind his back. "Let's go now," he commanded, and gave his prisoner a shove.

O'Grady walked to him, pausing to relieve the second man of his sidearm and nudge him forward. Smiling broadly, the Ranger put out his hand.

"Obliged, Patrick. That sucker put a ball in my shoulder. Oh, m'name's Bart Colter. Texas Rangers."

"Did you have any idea this man might have friends handy to help him?" O'Grady asked.

"Yep. The cap'n told me to be watchful."

"Why didn't he send along more men?"

"Didn't figger we needed to. We've got a story in the Rangers that sort of explains that. Seems there was this riot in Waco. It got real out of hand and the mayor sent to Austin for Rangers to stop the wanton destruction. Burt Thompson, who was chief Ranger at the time, wired back that help would arrive on the morning train. Next day the mayor and town marshal went down to the depot when the train came in. This young fella with a Ranger badge on his vest got off the train. 'Where's the rest of you?' the mayor asked. 'I'm it,' the Ranger said. 'There's been a mistake,' the mayor complained. 'We have a terrible riot on our hands.' The young Ranger looked at him and said, 'Yep. You've got one riot, we sent one Ranger.''

O'Grady chuckled appreciatively. "Whoever thought that one up has more imagination than's safe for any one man."

"Thing is, that's the way it happened. What say we take this pair down to the hoosegow?''

"Sure thing," O'Grady agreed.

When he finally reached his hotel room, O'Grady had no trouble falling into a deep sleep.

5

Dawn came to Eagle Pass and the new day passed slowly for Canyon O'Grady until nine-thirty, when the hoot of a train's steam whistle drew him out of boredom. He reached the depot in time to claim his baggage—two footlockers and a long flat case bound with iron straps, which he had purchased in San Antonio, along with some of the contents.

He employed his Irish charm to talk the stationmaster into allowing him to use a corner of the baggage room to sift through his belongings for items he felt he would need on the trail. He selected some clothing, two five-pound cans of FFFg powder, a large tin of five hundred percussion caps, and a custom-made box that contained five hundred of his specially cast conical bullets. Next he picked a tied bundle of soft cotton that contained fuse caps for blasting powder. These all went into the padded case that already held a Berdan long-range sharpshooter's rifle with telescope, chambered to fire the new Berdan .44-55 rimfire cased ammunition.

He then transferred additional clothing, camp cooking gear, and supplies to a single wooden footlocker and secured it. The depot agent agreed to let him leave everything there until he returned with a packhorse, which he intended to purchase when he retrieved Cormac from the livery stable.

By ten-forty-five, O'Grady had rigged all he would take onto the packsaddle, covered it with an oiled tarpaulin, and paid the clerk a small fee to keep his excess stored in the depot until his return. Already feeling the midmorning sun, he stepped into the saddle and swung Cormac's head to the south.

He crossed over the bridge into Piedras Negras to discover little changed from its counterpart in Texas. The streets might be a little dirtier, the signs all in Spanish, yet the flavor, the odor emanating from the saloons, the rowdy children spilling over the boardwalks into the street, all seemed alike.

His limited Spanish had a workout with the headline of a newspaper, *Hoy*, held out hopefully by a bright-eyed boy with an engaging smile. For twenty centavos he purchased a copy and worked out the meaning of the words, finding written language more difficult than spoken. Two more towns, Saucillo in Chihuahua and Santa Clara in Coahuila, had been added to the list of Colonel Death's victims.

A pattern had finally emerged, indicating that Kilgore led his men eastward, perhaps to the Sierra Madre Oriental. He could hide a force no larger than his in those mountains for years. If the mad colonel continued in that direction, it might be possible to intercept him by heading southward instead of to the southwest. His expression grim, O'Grady sought a way out of town that would lead due south. Kilgore could not be far ahead of him.

At the Plaza de Armas he noticed a young priest talking amiably with a group of children. The padre patted one lad on the head and fished a black silk ribbon from the pocket of his cassock. It had a Sacred Heart phylactery suspended from the middle. This he put over the boy's head and adjusted it around the neck. Then he blessed him and, laughing, the youngsters scampered off.

"Pardon me, Father," O'Grady tried his limited Spanish. "Can you tell me the shortest way to . . ." He considered a moment, recalling the last place listed as a victim of Colonel Death. "Santa Clara?"

"Certainly, my son." Quickly and efficiently the cleric described the route, pointed out the road, and wished O'Grady well.

O'Grady found the correct highway with ease. Putting the border towns behind him without regret, he started off into the semidesert country in a southeasterly direction.

On the outskirts of San Sebastián, Coahuila, in the foot-hills of the Sierra Madre Oriental, Colonel Kilgore and his command came up against an unexpected change in proce-dure. Prepared for a sweeping assault on the small village, the crescent formation of two ranks jerked to a halt at sight of a man sitting his horse at the wide gate in a low adobe wall that surrounded the town. He held aloft a shiny new Spencer rifle, a long strip of bed sheeting tied to the barrel.

"What next?" Captain Means asked rhetorically. "I've never heard of them giving up in advance. Not even these peons."

"Why don't we ride forward and see?" Colonel Kilgore suggested.

"Might be a trap," Sergeant Gruber warned.

"I don't think so. Look at the way he's dressed," the colonel differed.

In fact he could have been a Charro, or a wealthy land owner, mariachi, or a member of the Rurales. The similarity of dress hid subtle nuances to the eyes of the Americans. Colonel Kilgore and Captain Means rode forward. At a distance of some thirty feet, the emissary lowered his white flag.

"If you will stop right there, *señores*." His tone was casual, conversational, yet it held an edge of command. "My patron wishes to speak with you."

"You want to talk terms about the town?" Kilgore asked through Means's interpretation.

"Hardly, *señores*." A booming, affable voice, large enough to fill the space between, came from the direction of a stableyard.

Its owner, a man of small stature, yet possessed of a rich parade-ground voice, appeared out of the open stable door. He, too, carried a Spencer, the butt plate resting on one thigh. His clothing had an even more splendid quality than his subordinate's. He had overlarge hands and feet, and a pouter-pigeon chest, Kilgore noted as the stranger came closer.

"Allow me to introduce myself. I am Francisco Bernal, called El Carnicero by my friends and detractors alike. And you, of course, are Coronel Muerte."

Kilgore cocked a shaggy eyebrow. "My fame precedes me."

"Your infamy, *amigo*," the Butcher punned back. "You have come, no doubt, to sack San Sebastián. Unfortunately, I got here before you—I and my men, twenty-five excellent riders, deadly accurate marksmen, and jaguar-ferocious *bandidos*." Bernal chuckled warmly. "Or so we are labeled by the Rurales. We have done you the favor of relieving your men of the risk and—I regret having to say—the profit."

Eyes narrowing, Kilgore confronted the Butcher. "You feel you can best us in an open contest? A squadron of *lanzeros* tried and failed."

Bernal laughed heartily. "Probably not. We're not trained to fight as soldiers do. But who says we have to fight you openly or fairly? We know these hills, the mountains beyond. In the end you would lose."

"So what do you propose?" Kilgore asked, sensing some sort of compromise being offered.

"Why, that we join forces. You are—how you say?—notorious. You are also efficient. Your men understand the tactics of the *soldados*. There is much my men and I can learn from you, and much you can learn from us. What do you say? From what my eyes and ears along the road say, our numbers would double the size of your force. Is it a fair offer?"

"All of our men would share equally in the spoils of our efforts?" Kilgore asked.

"Done."

"Your subordinate leaders would be considered of equal rank to mine, if that's agreeable?"

"Absolutely."

"One thing. I am in command and I would remain in command after any such a merger. Captain Means, who is translating for us, is my adjutant. He would become executive officer and you would be adjutant. Is that acceptable?"

"*¡Hijo de la chingada! Yo . . .*"

"Son of a bitch," Means translated. "I set out to bring

you gringos to heel under my command and it is you who give the terms."

"We have a saying in our army," Kilgore said tightly. " 'Shit rolls off a leader's back. It only stains a coward.' "

Bernal slapped one thigh and bellowed his amusement. After a long, hearty peal of laughter he wiped at his streaming eyes with a big knuckle. *"Ya me gusta un hombre con cojones grandes."*

"I like a man with big balls," Means supplied.

"Pero ten cuidado que no acaben cortados," Bernal said coldly, drawling the last word, small, close-set eyes glittering.

"But be careful they don't get cut off."

"Jesus. So nice bargaining with him," Colonel Kilgore replied tightly. "Tell him this: I don't think a true friend would wield the knife."

El Carnicero's eyes widened and he snorted a guffaw through his ample nose. "Absolutely not!"

"Then we have an agreement?"

"Seguro."

Fifty-seven men strong, the combined forces of Colonel Judson Kilgore and Francisco Bernal rode out of San Sebastián after completing the looting and rape of the village.

For Canyon O'Grady the miles plodded by as the terrain steepened in gradient. Those solitary leagues gave him time to dwell on his assignment. For all that the newspapers were full of news of Colonel Death and his depredations, it still would not do for O'Grady to reveal his identity to the Mexican authorities. Given the evidence of their volatile humor in the past, they would probably consider his presence as another provocation. Or simply execute him as a spy. How had he come to make trouble his way of life?

Throughout childhood, "Trouble" might as well have been added to the list of Michael Patrick Canyon O'Grady's names. Not that he had evil in his heart, merely that he possessed a wild and rebellious spirit. That he had inherited from his father.

Liam O'Grady had fled to America to escape the English constabulary. As one of the founders of the Young Ireland Movement, he had had little choice. After the birth of his son, Canyon, Liam O'Grady took work with the railroad builders of the time, stretching the iron fingers of civilization through Massachusetts, New York, and Pennsylvania. By the time Canyon reached school age, he had lived in fifty-seven towns. The pattern didn't change.

No matter what village in western Massachusetts or Connecticut, upstate New York, or the still-untamed forests of western Pennsylvania the O'Grady family temporarily settled in, Canyon found himself in the middle of any mischief devised by the children of the community. Not only involved, but often leading it. His command extended not only to his contemporaries and younger boys but also to older lads as well.

Raised in a time when the peccadilloes of youth were considered annoying but tolerable, there wasn't an outhouse that got tipped over or moved while someone occupied the facility, nor flaxen tresses dipped in an inkwell that Canyon O'Grady had not been involved in. Many escapades, which later generations would consider heinous crimes, involved personal danger. Canyon O'Grady reveled in it. When Liam considered it wise to send him to Ireland, into the care of the wise and learned friars, Canyon soon involved himself in the activities of the Sinn Faine in overt resistance against England.

Once the good fathers found out, they put a quick end to it and he proceeded with his education. Back in the United States, after an eclectic view of past cultures, history, letters, and mathematics, Canyon found himself overqualified for many jobs that appealed to him. He could, of course, have taught at a university. But hell, he thought at the time, he was no older than many of the students. Instead, he sought adventure on the frontier. At that time, St. Louis was a far-flung outpost. Illinois still had not entered the Union, and the Cumberland Gap marked the jumping-off point from civilization to the wilderness. A lot had happened since then.

Ziii-crack!

Chilling in its sound and implication, the bullet that sped past O'Grady's ear terminated his search of the past. He dropped low on Cormac's neck and brought his attention fully to the front. A small village presented low, flat-roofed buildings to break the skyline. Another ball burned the air close by, and O'Grady slid off the saddle.

"Hey, what's going on?" he yelled at the invisible sniper.

"Go away. We want no gringos in our town."

O'Grady examined the village and saw no indication of destruction. Apparently Colonel Death had bypassed this community. He badly needed to replenish his water and have a hot meal and a good night's rest.

"I'm all alone. I'm only passing through," he forced into Spanish to reply.

"Keep away from us. No gringos. Go or we shoot better and kill you."

Shrugging, O'Grady waved his hat. "All right, all right, I'm going. No need to be testy now. I'll ride on out of sight, if you please." Tensed for a bullet to smash into his back, O'Grady put a foot in the stirrup and swung atop Cormac. "Steady, boy. Good horse," he crooned.

Taking up the lead rope to his packhorse, he put spurs to Cormac and trotted over a low swale and out of sight of the defensive little village. Many more like that, he reasoned, and he'd be in one hell of a fix.

Zaragoza, too, lay far enough north to be bypassed by Kilgore's freebooting horde. Tall ancient trees shaded the Plaza de Armas, and the populace went about their business peacefully. Off the plaza, on the south side of town, Canyon O'Grady located an inviting inn. Situated behind a low adobe wall, with high gateposts that supported the superstructure of an elaborate wrought-iron double gate, it reared three stories above its neighbors. A hand-carved wooden sign depicted a huge smiling sun, brightly painted, and above it letters that spelled: "LA POSADA DEL SOL."

The Inn of the Sun, O'Grady translated. It appeared to live up to its name. A flagstone patio fronted the establishment, long *ristras* of dried dark-red chiles hung from the Y-shaped support posts of the palm-leaf awning, and high double doors, again carved with the sun motif, provided access to the inner courtyard and registration desk. A small boy in faultlessly clean white cotton pants and shirt trotted up to his side.

"Sus caballos, señor?" He extended a hand for the reins.

"Ah—yes," O'Grady worked out in his limited Spanish. "Rub them down and grain them. Bring my gear on the packsaddle to the—ah—office."

"Sí, señor."

A small tile sign hung over a doorway cut into the passageway to the oasislike inner courtyard. *"Oficina,"* it said simply. O'Grady checked in and received the key to a room on the second floor. He'd only stepped into the tunnel when a vision of spectacular loveliness appeared from the area of the courtyard. Her full, well-molded lips moved into a friendly smile of greeting and she extended her hand for the key he held.

"Permit me, *señor*," she offered.

"Well . . . thank you." It was rare that O'Grady's famous Irish gift for words failed him.

He had been in hotels of all sorts, from three-to-a-bed stews to the most elegant. Never had he encountered so lovely a bellboy. Hardly a boy, he corrected himself. All those curves and bumps, and such a delightful wiggle to her behind. No, definitely not a boy. Service like this could become habit-forming.

At the room she unlocked the door and swung it wide, then entered after him. The sunny smile bloomed again. "Welcome to La Posada del Sol. *Cena* is served from twenty until twenty-three hours."

O'Grady did the mental shift to convert a twenty-four-hour clock to twelve. Dinner from eight to eleven. Much later than he would prefer. Still, different places, different customs. With siesta from one to five in the afternoon, few would want to dine early.

"If you would like a drink, the cantina is open. You can enjoy it there, or in the patio, or here in your room."

"The patio is quite inviting," O'Grady began, then considered his desire to be as unobserved as possible. He also noted a fleeting frown of . . . What? Disappointment? "But until I get baggage up here and situated, I think having it here would be better."

At once the alluring, provocative girl blossomed with smiles, dimples, and sparkling midnight eyes. "As you wish, *señor*. What will you drink? Beer? Tequila? Limonada?"

"Anything to get the trail dust out of my throat."

"Limonada, then. With tequila. I will bring it at once."

A few moments later a loud thumping caused O'Grady to bolt from the room. He had a clear image of the Mexican beauty taking a header down the stairwell. Instead he found the little stableboy dragging his footlocker up the stairs, thumping loudly on each riser. His moon face was squinched by effort and his *azotea* sandals threatened to skid out from under him with each mighty tug. His bright, liquid-chocolate eyes shone with pride in his accomplishment when he looked up at O'Grady.

"Only two more to go, *señor*," he chirped.

"I'll—ah—bring up the long flat one myself," O'Grady informed him, thinking of the precious telescope sight and the cotton-wrapped fuse caps.

When he returned to the room, the boy had already grabbed onto the second footlocker and begun the noisy journey to the second floor. The lad's task finished, O'Grady fished out a silver cartwheel peso coin and gave it to him. The boy's eyes widened.

"The *señor* is too generous. It is too much."

"Then split it with the hostler who has to tend my horses."

The boy blushed, then produced a rueful grin. "That is me also."

"So you have earned it, keep it."

And then the girl was there, dodging gracefully as the boy darted out. She carried a silver tray on which rested a tall black-painted clay bottle and two matching tiny cups. Also two greenish-cast blown-glass tumblers. Each of these contained a yellowish liquid. Small pottery dishes held salt and lime wedges. She set her burden on a small table and turned to O'Grady with a flourishing swirl of her multicolored skirt. Her white blouse, O'Grady noticed not for the first time, was T-shaped, with a large square opening for the bodice. A pattern of roses and twining vines had been embroidered around it.

"I thought we might enjoy a drink together," she said boldly.

"How is it you can get the time to spend with a guest? Is it your job?"

"No!" she answered hotly. "I am not a maid, nor a bar girl, nor a *puta*. I am Consuelo. So I have the time to do nearly anything I want."

O'Grady considered that. "*Con mucho gusto*, Consuelo. I am called Canyon O'Grady."

"*¿Cañon?* That is a name I have not heard before. How did you . . . ?"

" 'Twas my mother. She wanted a name for me that fitted the breadth and spirit of America." O'Grady launched into the familiar explanation. When he concluded, she looked at him with a mixture of amusement and awe.

"So then we shall be Consuelo and Canyon," she stated stoutly.

She turned to the beverages and began to pour cups of tequila. While she did, O'Grady took the opportunity to once more admire her petite, shapely figure, the large soft breasts that swelled behind the scant bodice, the fair, flawless complexion. With a toss of her long blue-black hair she turned back to him and extended a cup.

"You know how to drink it, yes?"

"Umm, just slug it down, I suppose."

"No-no, tequila must be savored. Come here, let me show you."

Consuelo went through the timeless ritual and O'Grady repeated it. After licking up the salt, biting the lime, and tossing off the half-ounce shot of tequila, O'Grady grimaced.

"You don't like?" Consuelo asked, disappointment clear in her words.

"Powerful stuff. Has an interesting flavor, though."

"Aha! Then what we must do is mix the tequila with limonada. That is generally considered a lady's drink, but we are here . . . alone . . . and no one will know."

Had she meant more than a discussion of drinks? O'Grady pondered it a moment. "Fine with me. Now, tell me, Consuelo, do you greet all of the inn's guests with so much personal attention?"

"Oh, no. Not . . . all of them."

She could well be nineteen or twenty, O'Grady considered, but her tiny size and angelic face made her appear more like sixteen. Now, that was one train of thought he determined to derail. She was a woman, not a girl. Up close, less than a forearm's distance between them, he could see the molded contours of maturity that assured this. He developed a beaming smile as he sipped at the mixed drink.

"Tasty," he declared it. "Would it be asking too much to invite you to share dinner with me?"

"I would be delighted. Here in your room? And what time?"

"I think the patio would be nice." O'Grady quickly noted her momentary flash of disappointment. "A secluded table, just the two of us. Say ni—twenty-one hours?"

"*Seguro*, Canyon. I . . . I will await the hour with anticipation."

Perusing again her alluring lines, planes, and curves, O'Grady felt his pulse increase. "So will I, lass. You can be sure of that."

6

Not for the dazzling company alone, Canyon O'Grady thought the evening's supper the best meal he had eaten in Mexico. In one corner of the inner courtyard, a mariachi band of three guitars, two violins, a pair of trumpets, and a small stringed instrument Consuelo told him was a Veracruz harp played sparkling music. Nearly every table was filled with guests of the posada or local persons of prominence. After the first hour of playing, the musicians circulated among the patrons, playing requests at tableside. When they came to the small out-of-the-way table where O'Grady and Consuelo sat shadowed by the broad ribbed leaves of a fan palm, Consuelo spoke up.

"May I?" At Canyon's nod, she made her request. "*Tocarle 'El Niño Perdido,' por favor.*"

Effusively the mariachis' leader rubbed pudgy hands together. "*Sí, patrona.* I will send for another trumpeter. Only a little minute and we can begin. In the meanwhile, would you wish another song?" He illustrated the length of the delay by holding a thumb and forefinger about an inch apart.

" '*La Golondrina,*' " Consuelo suggested.

"*Perfecto. Muchachos, 'La Golondrina.' Uno, dos . . .*"

After a brief introduction, the men's voices blended in haunting harmony, "*A-don-de va-a-a . . .*"

With casual absorption, which gave the gesture grace, Consuelo tapped a toe in time with the music. While the mariachis played, O'Grady noticed a stout individual with a wide expanse of belly and a bushy black mustache wending an apparently random path through the diners. The waxed facial hair had been carefully curled upward at the tips and waggled furiously as he volubly greeted well-known patrons. He reached the table where O'Grady sat with Consuelo as the music ended.

"So!" he boomed. "This is where I find you, eating up the profits with a first-time guest. What is a man to do?"

"Oh, Poppi, don't bluster so. You'll scare Canyon away and I do like him—er—his company."

"Poppi?" O'Grady gulped, already grasping that the large man had to be the owner of La Posada del Sol.

"Yes. She is my daughter," the portly proprietor replied in his dish-rattling voice. "I am Thomás Jiménez. You, I believe, are our *norteño* guest, Señor O'Grady."

"Yes, I am," O'Grady answered simply. "I had no idea . . . Consuelo . . ."

"Young people," Jiménez bellowed. "So good to be young again. Enjoy your evening. The night will be full of stars. Go on—go on, have your fun. It's not often I get to see my beloved Consuelo so happy. You two—eat, drink, talk, dance, laugh together. I will inform your waiter that the *cuenta* is mine."

After he departed, O'Grady turned a puzzled look to Consuelo. "The—ah—*cuenta*?

Her smile would have melted glaciers. "The check. Poppi is happy because I am happy. He's paying for our evening together. I think he likes you. I—ah—know I do."

Earlier, O'Grady had felt the strong stirring of desire and considered nothing beyond the usual appreciation for a good-looking woman expressing itself. Now the signals his groin sent held the urgency of awakening hunger for possessing Consuelo in ways far more intimate than those of the dance floor. Bearing in mind that he was in a foreign country, with different mores than those of the lusty frontier or the civilized East in his homeland, he worked at suppressing these erotic demands.

They remained, more powerful than before, at eleven o'clock when he escorted Consuelo to her door. He kissed her hand and agreed to meet for breakfast. After she had entered through the carved door, with an expression of longing, he turned away and started for his second-floor room. Quietly chuckling, O'Grady tried to convince himself he was being noble. He climbed the stairs and retired to the corner cubicle, where moonlight silvered the furnishings in alabaster beams that streamed through two high wooden-barred windows.

"You're a fool, O'Grady," he chided himself as he undressed and slid between crisp sheets. Head still filled with visions of Consuelo, he drifted off into sleep.

Soft scratching on his door awakened O'Grady with a start shortly after midnight. He came from the bed in knit jersey underdrawers, his Model '60 Colt ready in hand. At the portal, which still emitted a mouse-scrabble sound, he listened a moment, then abruptly opened it a crack.

Consuelo stood there, slender, pale, feet bare, and a wraparound robe of some gauzy material that highlighted more of her delightful body than it concealed. The hem ended well above her ankles. Her eyes were large and doe-like, limpid circles like strong black coffee.

"I . . . had to come," she whispered.

"I'm glad you did," O'Grady answered back, relieved that he had no need for the gun. "Saved me the trouble of coming after you."

He swung the door wide and she entered in a rush. On tiptoe she put her arms around his neck while he closed the door. They kissed, long and deeply, her oblivious of the hard metal-and-wood pressure of the Colt's butt against the small of her back.

Consuelo drank of him, consumed and gave back in ample measure. O'Grady's arousal was immediate and compelling. His risen member pressed insistently against her lower abdomen. Moaning, she ground her pubic mound into its rigid bulk. He twisted his mouth away from hers and air gusted out of it as though he had sustained a solid blow to the solar plexus.

"Oh, Canyon—Canyon, I was dying for the need of you," Consuelo panted.

"And I, you," O'Grady returned, and found he was telling the truth.

His sleep had been restless, shallow. His hunger for this pliant, vibrant body had kept him on the edge of slumber. Reluctantly he released her, the thick fingers of one big hand seeking the tie-belt of her robe. Her tiny hand sought his chest, ran down it, thrilling to the sparse spray of russet hairs that bristled there. It slid lower, over the hard plates of his belly muscles, paused at the drawstring waist of his underdrawers. With a happy little sound she dipped fingers below the cloth and sought out his throbbing phallus.

"Oh!" she squeaked. "Oh, my. *Muy grande, muy guapo*." She sucked air through her teeth as O'Grady undid her cloth belt and let the robe fall free.

In pale moonlight her firm, full breasts seemed globes of ivory. His hard, callused hands cupped them as she encircled his manhood with eager fingers. His thumbs kneaded the pert nipples, demanding greater hardness of them as they responded to his attentions.

"This is quite a bit more than I expected from a supper invitation," O'Grady said lightly.

"And *this* is a whole lot more than I expected," Consuelo teased, giving his rigid shaft a playful squeeze.

His hands left her generous bust, followed the flare of her rib cage, darted down and inward to her narrow waist, flowed outward with the flare of her hips, then down to cup her firm round bottom. Quickly Consuelo untied the underwear string and O'Grady's drawers dropped to the floor around his ankles. Slowly Consuelo sank to her knees and her silken cheek caressed the sensitive tip of O'Grady's organ. He shivered in delight and she inclined backward far enough to let her soft, mobile lips brush the same area in a warm, moist kiss.

At a light touch from O'Grady, she came to her feet and he lifted her in his arms, held her close to him, his member hard and compelling, and carried her with ease to the waiting bed. There he peeled her out of the wrap and they embraced, jangled by the delirious sensation of bare flesh blending into oneness.

Eagerly Consuelo left his embrace to arrange herself invitingly on the bed. O'Grady joined her and his hands did magic things, drawing forth coos and sighs of increasing ardor. Her own fingers kept busy, touching, stroking, squeezing. When neither of them could bear to prolong the delirious exploration, O'Grady insinuated himself between her widespread legs.

Slowly he lowered his turgid organ until it met her fevered cleft, which welcomed him with open petals. With infinite care he inserted a portion of his endowment and Consuelo shivered in delight. Small though powerful contractions began to draw him deeper. He gave in to this noteworthy technique and allowed himself to be ingested until he hilted in a splendorous collision of pubic arches.

"*Ay, corozón*, love me, love me now," Consuelo panted.

Long, powerful strokes brought her to completion twice before O'Grady sensed the building pressure of his fulfillment. Arms and legs twined around his neck and waist, Consuelo clung to him as he relentlessly crescendoed in splintering light and celestial music.

"Ooh, Canyon, never, never has it been so lovely. I've not known many men, *amado*, and those few have never been so much. Can we . . . will we do it again?"

Delighted by the stupendous experience, O'Grady answered lightly, "If we don't, we'll regret it the rest of our lives. I intend to take very good care of you tonight."

In the state of Nuevo León, at the village of Reata, in the foothills of the Sierra Madre Oriental, Colonel Judson Kilgore sat in the well-appointed office of the former mayor, recently deceased. He sipped a brandy and reflected on their accomplishments so far. Outside, his men and those of Francisco Bernal plundered and raped their way to satiety. They had accumulated a remarkable store of valuables, gold, silver, and paper currency. For which only eleven men, total, had been killed, with but three wounded beyond active participation. His observations had a dark side also.

Ammunition was running low. Not dangerously so, yet enough to prompt him to issue an order to scavenge all the usable calibers of ball and all the powder possible from the towns they looted. Likewise suitable feed for the horses grew short in supply. Although the hour was late, Kilgore didn't find it unusual when an orderly knocked on the door.

"Three Mezkin, ah, gentlemen to see you, Colonel."

"What do they want?"

"Not sure, sir. Said they had to talk to you."

"Send them in."

When the trio entered, Kilgore took in the expensive finery they wore, the heavy gold rings on many fingers, good quality boots. They stopped three paces from the desk and, to Kilgore's surprise, clicked heels and bowed.

"Permit me, Señor Coronel, to introduce my companions and myself. The gentleman on my left is Don Gustavo Agilar, formerly the *haciendado* of Rancho Santa Verónica de Chihuahua. To my right is Don Hernán de Vega. He is the former imperial governor of Monterrey. And I have the honor to be Don Alfonso Brisa. My holdings included a large portion of the southern half of Coahuila."

"Pardon the delay, I will send for my interpreter so that we may use your accustomed language. Orderly, summon Captain Means."

"Yes, sir."

"Now, gentlemen, I am Colonel Judson Kilgore."

Means stepped into the office in time to translate Brisa's comments. "Ah, yes, the one called Coronel Muerte. It is why we come to you."

"What do you expect me to do?" Kilgore snapped. He had little sympathy for these strutting, posturing imperialists. They had betrayed their own country to collaborate with the French in stripping Mexico of wealth Kilgore considered rightfully his own.

Tactfully Means translated the demand to "Have you gentlemen had time to refresh yourselves since arriving at our headquarters?"

"Certainly," Brisa answered with a gesture of denial.

"Actually, no," Hernán de Vega injected. "We have been hiding in this wretched village for two weeks. There has been little food and a lot of danger. Had we been discovered, we would have gone to the firing wall."

Means explained to Kilgore, including the proper protocol for conducting business in Mexico. Not liking it, Kilgore nevertheless put on his company manners.

"Well, then, we should have a little something to restore you." He called to the orderly to send for the cantinero of the next-door saloon.

When that worthy arrived, rubbing his pudgy hands together in trepidation, Kilgore issued crisp orders. "Bring us some food, something substantial, and a couple of bottles of good wine."

Kilgore offered chairs and through Means made small talk until the bar owner returned with two waiters and large trays of food. He produced two dusty bottles of Domecq red wine and bowed his way out after opening them. At Kilgore's invitation the starving imperialists set to on the fat tamales, savory chunks of open-fire-roasted pork, and a half-dozen condiments. When they reached the *pan dulce* and brandy poured by Captain Means, Kilgore forged into the business at hand.

"I understand that you have endured considerable discomfort since last year when Maximilian was deposed. No doubt your fellow countrymen are not kindly disposed toward you. What, though, do you expect I can do about it?"

"We had hoped . . . that is, Coronel, we would like . . ." Brisa stammered.

"Coronel Kilgore, you have a strong, well-trained force that has been able to sweep over all opposition so far," de Vega injected smoothly. "You have even enlisted the loyalty of a notorious *bandido*, Francisco Bernal. It is our intention to throw in our lot with you."

A patronizing smile curled Kilgore's full lips. A lot of good that would do. Three graying men and a handful of servants. "Tell me, then, how would I benefit from this?"

De Vega made a deprecating gesture. "I was an officer in the war between your country and mine. Although we lost, I can modestly say that I served with distinction and acquitted my troops and myself well on the battlefield. I could offer myself in such a capacity again."

"I am not a military man," Brisa offered, fingers laced over his brocaded vest. "But I am an accountant. I would imagine you are in need of someone to catalog your—ah—acquisitions?"

"That's so," Kilgore allowed.

His voice a high squeak compared to his companions', Gustavo Agilar contributed his qualifications. "I served as captain of a company of *lanzeros* under his imperial majesty, Maximilian. We fought well, until all resources had been exhausted."

"We are no longer rich men," de Vega summed up. "And we understand running an army of this sort takes a lot of money. What we have managed to salvage, we have converted into cash. There is that, and our retainers."

A few thousand pesos and a dozen or so untried servants, Kilgore interpreted their offer again. "What exactly, are we speaking of here?"

"Combined, we have some one hundred eighty thousand pesos," de Vega said slowly. "And thirty heavily armed, battle-experienced men."

"My . . . God," Kilgore let slip before he could cut it off. He turned a questioning glance on Lance Means.

Incredulous, Captain Means stared blankly at the trio of

imperialists. If that was being poor, what the hell was being rich to these men? At his superior's interrogative expression, he made an impreceptible nod.

Recovering himself, Kilgore beamed. "Well, gentlemen, I think we can say welcome to the army of Coronel Muerte."

Shortly before dawn, Consuelo slipped from O'Grady's bed and padded barefoot back to her own quarters. He awakened, shaved and dressed, took a scant breakfast of hot chocolate, sweet rolls, and fruit, then finished with coffee. Little Pablo, the stableboy, helped him saddle the horses. He left the lad another silver peso and rode off to the east.

He felt it better that way. Had he waited to join Consuelo for breakfast, odds were his desire would win out over duty and he would spend at least another night in the rhapsody at the Inn of the Sun. With Cormac and the packhorse refreshed, he made good time.

By three-thirty he could make out the skyline of Sabinas, Coahuila, where newspaper reports indicated Kilgore had made his most recent raid in that state. The sun at his back, O'Grady rode into town. He progressed for three blocks before he saw any sign of the damage done.

Bullet holes pockmarked the white-plastered walls of adobe buildings along the street, and here and there the rust-brown stains of dried blood remained as grim reminders. By the time he reached the Plaza de Armas, a fair collection of youngsters trotted in his wake. One darted ahead of his fellows and offered to take O'Grady's horses.

"*Bueno,*" O'Grady responded, using his slowly increasing Spanish. "There's fifty centavos in it for you. If you see they are stabled and given grain, another fifty centavos."

Eyes wide in expectation, the boy nodded and trotted away with the animals. O'Grady retained his saddlebags, which he draped over his left shoulder. Across the way he saw a promising cantina. Several stores had been burned out and there were broken windows, though little else to indicate the depredations that had occurred. O'Grady entered the cantina and stepped to the bar.

At his feet he noted the urinal trough that he surmised to be part and parcel of every bar in Mexico. "*Cerveza, por favor,*" he placed his order.

He had taken two swallows when he noticed the hard

looks of the men around him. Resentment of Americans had always run high, so he dismissed it. He had the tall, slender glass—a *tubo* in Mexican saloon parlance—to his lips for another swallow when the tall carved wood front doors slammed open and a high-pitched voice yelled to all and sundry, "There he is! That's the *gringo ladrón*. He's one of them, come back to hurt us again."

Seven persons pushed their way into the bar behind the accuser. They rushed at O'Grady with grim determination. The ruddy-haired government agent considered drawing his Colt and ending it right fast. Then, to his immediate regret, he dismissed the thought.

A fist slammed into his rib cage. Not a fierce blow, only an irritant, so that he was able to fling away the small assailant. Two more punches hit his face, and a shrimp of a fellow worried at one of his legs as if to throw him off balance. In an eye-blink O'Grady detected that his tormentors were all children. Boys in their early teens, to be exact. Realization caused him to look up in time to catch a huge hard fist in the face.

That punch staggered him, sent him reeling along the bar. O'Grady recovered and sought the source of his battering. A bear of a man in leather apron and rolled-up sleeves hung on the fringe of the agitated youngsters. O'Grady batted a couple more away and the big fellow—he had to be the blacksmith, O'Grady surmised—swung another powerful blow.

It caught O'Grady under his left eye. Hampered by the swarm of juveniles, he had been unable to dodge. Unleashing his own cocked right, he popped the blacksmith in the nose. He felt a satisfying crunch of cartilage.

Blood began to stream down the huge man's upper lip. He blinked, as though in disbelief, shook his head, and waded in again. Sharp pain alerted O'Grady to a new threat.

With little canine growls, a slight lad of twelve or so set his teeth in O'Grady's right thigh and began to worry his head from side to side. O'Grady used a handful of coarse black hair to prize the biter free and dodged another slashing attack of white teeth. He shoved the youths into each other's arms and sent them spinning away from the bar.

Relieved of that danger, he raised his gaze in time to see up close a set of four big callused knuckles speeding toward his forehead. Vaguely, as though from a distance, he heard the crunch of contact and a hot, sharp pain pierced his brain. Then O'Grady melted into blackness.

7

At least he had awakened on earth, O'Grady considered calmly, his eyes still closed. The sour odor of old vomit and the ammonia aroma of stale urine convinced him of that, also that his surroundings were hardly of the most elegant. He opened his eyes to blackness. Gradually the dim light of stars illuminated a small window high in the wall, with round vertical bars filling the opening. He made to sit up, and groaned.

"Well, boy-o, you're back with the living, I see."

A cornhusk mattress rustled and O'Grady sensed the presence of the other man, hovering over him. A cool hand touched his forehead. For a moment it gave relief; then a stab of pain pierced his skull from the bruise. With that, he remembered.

"I was in the cantina. A big ox of a man hit me right between the running lights," O'Grady stated in hopes of enlightenment.

"That's be Oscar Cervantes, the blacksmith. Got a punch on him would fell a bull. M'name's O'Marra, Carlos O'Marra."

"Canyon O'Grady. I thought I detected a bit of the lilt of Dublin in your voice."

"By inheritance only. My father is from the Auld Sod, but me mother is the third daughter of a hidalgo, and thus not of political or financial advantage for a proper society match. Yet fair enough for my sire to marry. My full name reads like a whole family, Carlos Jesús y María Fernando O'Marra y Bustamante."

"That's a mouthful. Wha . . . where are we?"

"Why, in the *carcel*, boy-o. The lockup, the sink."

"Jail?"

"None other. What did they put you here for?"

"I . . . don't know. Some kids in the cantina, sprats not much more than thirteen or so, and one of them said, 'That's the one,' and the fight started.

"Ummm. Must be because you're a gringo. After the good Colonel Death came through, these folks haven't much affection for Yanquis."

"I'm not one of them. I just got here."

"In their minds, it's one and the same, boy-o," O'Marra told him.

"I'm only riding through."

"Where to?"

In the subdued light of the cell, O'Grady took on a brooding expression barely seen by his companion. "To— ah—well, to Nuevo León."

"That's the way ol' Colonel Death headed. So that makes you doubly guilty in their eyes."

"What can I do to get out of here?" O'Grady appealed.

"Truth is, there's not a hell of a lot. Unless, of course, you have considerable money and are willing to part with some of it."

"How do you mean?" O'Grady asked, not positive, though suspecting where this conversation would lead.

"*Mordida*, man. The bite, the squeeze, the payoff." O'Marra paused and sighed heavily. "Look, there are only two classes in Mexico. The rich and the poor, the peons. Although he was born a poor Indian boy, Benito Juárez is now President of Mexico and a wealthy man. There are few ways to rise from the bottom. Politicians, the military, the big land owners, even bandits live better than the peons. And *mordida* is the grease that keeps the wheels turning.

"Outside of the very rich, no one is paid enough. They are expected to make up the difference through bribes offered for their favor. The only ones who don't have some-one to extract bribes from are the peons, except for a few pure-blood Indians in the mountains to the south. It's not right, it's not fair, but it is the way things are. Juárez wants to change all that, and he nearly got himself assassinated for suggesting it. So, if you are able to handle the *mordida*, odds are you can get out of here fairly easily."

A nerve-grating discordant clack sounded from outside the cell window. O'Grady winced. "What's that?"

"Next door is the cathedral. It has a clock in the bell tower which tells the quarter-hour, half-hour, and hour. Thing is one bell's cracked and the others were poorly cast. Make a terrible racket."

O'Grady stifled another groan. "All I want now is for my head to quit aching so I can get some sleep."

"Tomorrow, boy-o," O'Marra urged. "Wait and see how things go tomorrow."

All through the night, O'Grady's throbbing head received no succor from the cracked, flat-sounding bells in the church next door to the jail as they produced cacophonous tocsins to announce the passage of time. Another agony joined the rest shortly after daylight. It sounded to his punished ears like someone dropping all the metal in a steam locomotive down a flight of stairs.

"*¡Despertarse! ¡Despertarse!*" an inordinately fat jailer bellowed as he walked along the main corridor, slamming the bars with a hickory nightstick.

He turned the corner into O'Grady's cellblock and continued the abuse. When he reached their cell, he stopped and produced a big ring of keys. Leering, he unlocked the door and swung it wide.

"Come out of the cell," he commanded.

"Now what?" O'Grady inquired.

"We'll soon find out," O'Marra commented with a shrug.

In daylight, dim though it was inside the jail, O'Grady saw a man who, at first glance, might easily be taken for a native. His brown face and hands protruded from the usual white cotton shirt and trousers and he wore *azoteas* on his bare, tawny feet. The only jarring elements were his sandy hair and gold-flecked blue eyes. The jailer gave them shoves in the direction of the main corridor.

They needed no urging to get a move on, and walked smartly ahead of the guard. He directed them to the big metal-cased door that separated the cellblocks from the guardroom and the chief's office beyond. There he unlocked the portal and swung it open. Inside they were told to clean themselves and scrape the beard from their faces.

O'Grady saw his packsaddle and other gear stacked in one corner. It appeared that no one had tampered with any of it. Considering the explosives and telescoped rifle, he felt a momentary swirl of relief. A clay basin of cold water and bar of hard soap waited him.

"Court day," O'Marra advised.

"You're sure?"

"Oh, yes." He sniffed. "Smell that, boy-o? The rotten stench of jail food. They wouldn't be feeding us out here if we weren't goin' to court."

When they finished, O'Grady found places set for them at a table. Tin plates held a day-old rock-hard bread roll— a *bolillo*, O'Marra informed him—a dab of watery grease-scummed beans, and a galvanized egg. Metal cups held an acrid, watery brew the sandy-haired O'Marra laughingly called coffee.

"Remember what we were talking about last night?" he asked rhetorically. "Well, if you've the money, you can buy anything you want to eat. To drink too. Even get a hot little *puta* in here to warm your bed and haul your ashes."

"Remarkable," O'Grady said dryly.

Flat clangs announced the steady passing of each fifteen minutes. An hour and a half after being brought out of their cell, O'Grady and O'Marra remained seated, bored and unenlightened. As the clock bells in the church started to discordantly fracture the hour of nine o'clock, a short barrel-shaped man with gimlet eyes and a small greedy mouth entered.

"Carlos O'Marra?" he inquired.

"That's me," O'Marra acknowledged, standing.

"I am Esteban Villareal. I will be your *abogado*. Come with me."

"*Sí, señor abogado.*" To O'Grady he spoke in English. "Wish me luck."

Justice appeared to move swiftly in Mexico, O'Grady observed when Carlos O'Marra returned in less than thirty minutes. The Mexican-Irishman had a big grin spread on his face and walked with a much lighter tread than when he had departed.

"I got fined a hundred pesos for disorderly conduct, that's the knuckle-scraper I told you I was in outside the cantina, and have to do three more days in jail."

"You're smiling over that?" O'Grady asked, confused.

"I could have been sentenced to three months' hard labor."

"You are the *norteño*, Señor Patterson?" Villareal asked in a nasty tone.

"Patrick, mister."

"I am also to be your attorney. Come with me."

"Just a minute. My Spanish isn't all that good. I'd like someone with me so I know what is going on. Will you do it, O'Marra?"

"Glad to, boy-o."

Villareal and the fat jailer exchanged glances; then the rotund little attorney beckoned to O'Marra. Off to one side they held a short whispered conversation, O'Marra either objecting or bargaining. Finally he turned to O'Grady.

"Here's where the bite comes in. They want two hundred pesos to let me be your interpreter."

Shocked, O'Grady blurted, "Where're their masks and guns?"

"It's the way things are, O'Grady," O'Marra told him simply.

Although he had apparently been searched for weapons, his boot knife was missing, his money had not been touched. Now he knew why. Grudgingly he delved into a pocket of his whipcord trousers and produced four fifty-peso gold pieces. These he handed to O'Marra, who gave them to the lawyer. Villareal in turn passed along one fifty-peso coin to the jailer, who scowled in disapproval.

"Come with me," Villareal commanded.

Outside the jail, two lean young men in tan uniforms fell in at O'Grady's sides. Each held a rifle at high port in a competent manner. On the side of the jail, opposite the cathedral, stood the Edificio Municipal. Following the lawyer's lead, O'Grady walked that direction. Tall, wide wrought-iron gates with a fan-shaped grillwork above barred the entranceway outside of business hours. Now they stood open, a uniformed guard at each side. The tall, tunnellike passage rose to two full stories.

Beyond it a flagstone-paved courtyard presented a drab vista. An empty fountain that listed slightly to one side held a collection of last fall's discarded leaves. Three stunted trees struggled for survival along the longer wall opposite. At the far end, the plastered surface of the inner-facing wall had been pockmarked by numerous bullet holes. The dark rust stains at the base left little doubt as to what purpose the grim partition served. O'Marra noticed the source of O'Grady's preoccupation.

"It's called *el paredón*, the firing wall. They're quite serious about its use."

"You're a wealth of comfort and encouragement," O'Grady riposted tight-lipped.

"It's usually reserved for political prisoners. Although I suppose that's what you'll be considered."

"Are you finished with it, man?" O'Grady snapped.

Except for the judge's bench, the courtroom bore little resemblance to any Canyon O'Grady had ever seen. Beyond the bar, the low wooden rail-top fence that separated the spectator area from the legal arena, no chairs had been provided for the defendant or his counsel. Instead a small lectern provided a resting place for notes. The prosecution had an ample table, comfortable chairs, and a tabletop podium from which to address the bench. A wizened man in shirtsleeves and a green eyeshade, whom O'Grady rightly figured to be the recorder, sat directly in front of the tall, glowingly polished edifice that formed the judge's dais.

To the left, looking at the bench, a raised and enclosed hexagonal platform, like a pulpit, provided space for witnesses to testify. At a halfway elevation on the right sat the clerk. At their entry, a uniformed officer, the bailiff, began bawling his ritual.

"All those having business before the honorable Judge Arturo Montalbán gather near and observe silence. Judge Arturo Montalbán, presiding in the Prefecture Court of Coahuila."

If the jailer could be called fat, Judge Montalbán made the word insignificant. He lived up to his name, truly a mountain of a man, so grossly obese that he had to turn sideways to fit through the doorway behind the bench. His black robe and white cap of office only emphasized his size. He was corpulent to the point of waddling when he walked, and his hawkish Indian features, coarse pockmarked skin, and small beady eyes, which bore a perpetual squint, signaled to O'Grady the avaricious corruption below the oily, polished exterior.

When the flabby judge settled himself into his chair, which creaked in protest, he flicked a quick glance at the clerk. That worthy rose and read aloud from a sheet of paper in his hand.

"The State of Coahuila versus Michael Patrick, a vagrant alien."

Judge Montalbán peered myopically at the defendant and his counsel, then settled his gaze on Carlos O'Marra. "Ah, Señor O'Marra, I see you are back in this court. Didn't you see enough of it the last time?"

O'Marra explained his reason for being there. The judge scowled and motioned for O'Marra and Villareal to come forward. O'Grady noticed that so far no prosecutor had made an appearance. A brief whispered conversation followed, and then O'Marra and the lawyer returned.

"The judge has assessed a fee of three hundred pesos for the privilege of using an interpreter," the sandy-haired young man explained. "More *mordida*. You'll have to pay up or Montalbán will throw me out of court."

"Thieving bastard," O'Grady growled. He produced the money, which O'Marra took forward. O'Grady spoke to his attorney. "Where is the prosecutor?"

Villareal looked puzzled, then surprised. "Why, there won't be one. The judge has the prosecution's case before him on paper."

"What about witnesses? Don't I get to face my accusers?"

Villareal shrugged. "What for? I have heard that in your law you have that quaint custom. But here, we follow the code of Napoleon, in that you are guilty until proved innocent."

A terrible chill ran along O'Grady's spine. Judge Montalbán interrupted before he could question his lawyer further. "Señor Villareal, are you ready to put on a defense?"

"Not at this time, Juez Montalbán. I have only met my client."

"You know I will not tolerate delays, *compadre*. Say what you have to say and get done with it."

"Oh, damn," O'Marra added to his translation. "I wish I had known that before."

"What?" O'Grady appealed.

"The judge is apparently godfather to one or more of the children of our fine attorney here. It doesn't look good, boy-o."

"What's that all about?" Judge Montalbán snapped, eager for another reason to collect a bribe.

"I was explaining our judicial system to my friend here," O'Marra lied smoothly.

"Enough of that. I repeat, what defense do you have to put on?"

Clearing his throat harshly, Villareal drew himself up to his inconsiderable height and spoke in a nasal whine. "This gringo—ah—the defendant claims to be riding through, whatever that means. He says he has never seen the man called Coronel Muerte and is definitely not a part of his gang of bandits. That's all."

Angry at this slipshod treatment of his defense, Canyon O'Grady bristled and raised a strong voice, vibrant with outrage. "No, it is not all. Sabinas was raided four days ago. Four days ago I had just arrived in Zaragoza. It's impossible for me to be in two places at once. I stayed there at La Posada del Sol. Your honor, in all fairness, all you need do is continue this trial a few days while you send for verification of that."

Judge Montalbán's pudgy features screwed up into a mask of malignant hate and he leaned forward, resting his bulk on balloon hands. "There is no need to waste time like that. I find your spurious reasoning totally illogical and an insult to this court. The facts are in evidence. You are a gringo, no? You carry guns. So it is obvious that you are one of Coronel Muerte's murderers. Since there is no witness who can definitely connect you with any specific killing, I am compelled to leniency."

"Of course there's no witness. I wasn't here, dammit!" O'Grady shouted.

"Another outburst like that and I'll also find you in contempt of court. *Compadre*," he addressed Villareal, "admonish your client to conduct himself in an orderly fashion."

"*Sí, compad*—er—Juez Montalbán." The little man turned to O'Grady, craning his neck to look the six-footer in the eye. "Behave yourself. The evidence is in, the judge has made up his mind. All that remains is the sentencing."

"My . . . God," O'Grady said with sagging jaw.

"There being no further testimony, it is the duty of this court to pronounce sentence. Since there is no evidence to connect you to one given killing, I sentence you to five years' hard labor and a fine of five hundred thousand pesos."

"Not even God has half a million pesos," O'Grady yelled before he could control himself.

A bleak, wintry smile spread over Montalbán's thin, bloodless lips. "Then you shall serve time in lieu of the money, at a rate of five pesos a day. Take him away." As guards closed in on O'Grady, the judge announced, "Next case."

8

Incessant and irritating, the insipid bell chimed the quarter-hour. Midnight had come and gone. Canyon O'Grady lay sleepless on the adobe ledge that formed his bunk, hands behind his head. Across from him, O'Marra stirred.

"Time has come for another practical lesson in *mordida*, boy-o," he whispered to his cellmate.

"Meaning what, this time? A few more of your lessons and I'll be broke. Not that it matters with half a million pesos' fine to pay."

"As you said to the judge, not even God has half a million pesos, boy-o. Not since the Frenchies looted the national treasury and everyone since has helped himself to whatever he could find. No, this is far more practical than trying to buy that judge. How much have you got with you?"

O'Grady considered it. He could find no logical reason why the police and the bailiff had not stripped him of every cent right in the courtroom. He still had plenty on him. Not counting what he had sequestered in his gear on the packsaddle. Yet he hedged at revealing how much money had been provided by the President for this assignment.

"I've about six hundred in gold on me," he advised.

"Should be more than enough," O'Marra assured him. Standing now, he pressed his face to the bars. "*¡Oye, carcelero!*" he yelled.

He kept on until there came an angry mutter. Locks

clacked and steel doors rattled. The jailer approached yawning, his uniform rumpled. It was not the fat man who had awakened them, O'Grady noted. This one had a ferret face and gimlet eyes. He *looked* greedy and ready for a bribe.

"What do you want now? It's the middle of the night," he complained to O'Marra.

"My friend here has a little something for you," O'Marra responded.

They conducted a low-voiced conversation for an interminable minute. Then O'Marra turned, smiling. He put out his hand and gestured with the universal sign for money, rubbing his thumb and forefinger together. He silently mouthed, "Two hundred, U.S."

O'Grady frowned and sat on the edge of his bunk. That came to three thousand, four hundred pesos, a veritable fortune. He removed his boot and, from a small pouch tied above his ankle, removed ten double eagles. These he handed to O'Marra. The turnkey sucked in his breath in astonishment at the faint, soft glint of gold in the dim light of the corridor. O'Marra passed the money on to him. A rhapsodic smile lifted the corners of the guard's mouth.

Keys appeared and their magic tinkle accompanied the unlocking of the door. *"Muchas gracias, señor gringo,"* he lisped quietly.

Then he walked to the far end of the corridor and unlocked a rear door. Still sporting the ear-to-ear smirk, he came past the cell and on to the cross corridor. He turned and padded along it to the thick wood-and-metal partition separating the cellblock from the guardroom. In moments it boomed closed behind him.

"Meaning I'm free?" O'Grady asked quietly.

"Like the darlin' birds," O'Marra told him.

"Considering the wide general practice of bribery, I can only wonder if our jailer is an honest crook."

"Whatever do you mean?"

"Simple, O'Marra. An honest crook is one who, once he has been bought, stays bought."

"A remarkable observation, boy-o. Taken in that light, what do you have in mind?"

"I thought we might slip out the front, instead of the convenient way the turnkey set up. Wouldn't do to be shot while trying to escape."

"You've a truly devious mind, O'Grady, an' that's a fact," O'Marra said in appreciation and awe.

"Good, then. Let's get on our way."

"I'm overwhelmed by your assurance that I am going with you."

"Only so far as out of here," O'Grady told him. "I wouldn't be so coldhearted as to leave you here to take the brunt of it when it's discovered I'm gone. Outside of here, we're both on our own. Now, take off your boots."

"What for?"

"For quiet, man. Do you want to make enough noise to wake the dead?"

Carlos O'Marra nodded his understanding and both men removed their boots. On silent feet they made their way along the cellblock to the intersection with the main corridor. Several uneasy prisoners awakened and made to speak, until O'Marra silenced them with a gesture. The door they found unlocked, much to O'Grady's surprise.

Beyond the portal, three men snored away the early-morning hours in rough, handmade wooden bunks. A fourth, their jailer, sat in a high-back swivel chair behind a desk. The slow, deep, steady rhythm of his breathing satisfied O'Grady that the turnkey likewise snoozed. The President's agent hefted one of the hickory billies and swung it with barely sufficient force. It made a hollow *klonk* against the side of the dozing policeman's head and O'Grady nodded in satisfaction.

He mimed looking for objects and they soon found their firearms, personal property, and the still-rigged packsaddle with all of O'Grady's supplies. It took two trips to lug it all onto the street. Through it all, the three jail keepers slept blissfully in their bunks.

"He'll have a hell of a lump in the morning," O'Grady observed of the unconscious jailer.

Outside they found the streets deserted. "This way," O'Marra urged. "They will have put your horses in the livery stable."

Two blocks passed in silence before O'Grady offered a studied conjecture. "You know, I sort of think the jail warden wanted us to go out that way. He left the door unlocked, and he had a happy smile on his face when I thumped him with that nightstick."

"Sure an' you may have the right of it there. This way

he has something to show his superiors to prove he wasn't involved in the escape. And maybe he can keep the whole bribe for himself. Now, once we're saddled up, which way will we be headin'?"

O'Grady suddenly found himself with a partner. One thing he decidedly did not want to have. "Where do you come up with the 'we'? Did you bring that little lawyer, Villareal, along in your hip pocket?"

"Bucko, you need an interpreter. At least for a while, until you're free of these people who have had a run-in with our Colonel Death. As a Mexican and a citizen of the country, I'll be listened to far more than you."

He had to admit the reasonableness of that, O'Grady concluded. For a while, at least. Through constant necessity, his Spanish improved daily. He swung around the corner of the livery and headed for a side door.

"We're going to Nuevo León."

"Jesus, you are after that crazy bastard, aren't you?"

"Nothing like that," O'Grady told him simply.

Nature had twisted and folded the Sierra Madre Oriental in such a manner that the villages and hamlets located there might be no farther apart than five miles by the flight of the proverbial crow, yet invisible to each other and up to twenty miles by road. It did serve to increase the number of places to loot and ravage.

At first, Colonel Judson Kilgore relished the swift, easy additions to his treasure. It had grown now to the point that four wagons carried the chests of coin, paper currency, and the gold and silver gleaned from churches. His present occupation had given Kilgore a new appreciation of the Church of Rome.

At least they still did things the old way. Heavy gold chalices, gold patens for the Host, silver bells, silver holders for the ampullae of water and wine—even the poorest parish church yielded up these. Thick gold leaf, applied to alter faces and statues of saints, produced more wealth. It took a lot of it, he thought grimly, just to keep his army together.

So far they had seized enough food to provide. What he would do about that when the time came that they couldn't, remained to be seen. Lance Means was working on that. Kilgore had another issue, brought to him by some of his original command, that demanded his full attention. His own awareness of the situation only added to the urgency of a solution.

He sat his big bay in the Plaza de Armas in San Juan Bautista, observing, rather than participating, in order to come to some decision. A small child ran screaming across the wedge of grass to one side. He dodged to put a tree between him and his pursuer.

Grinning broadly, the short, swarthy, onetime Mexican bandit closed on the fleeing youngster. He raised his arm and the machette he held flashed in the morning sunlight. It descended and made a solid chunk as he severed the head from the lad's neck.

"You don't need . . ." Colonel Kilgore started, then checked himself. To a man his Mexican recruits were a volatile lot. Butchering children when it wasn't necessary didn't sit well with him, but these men had a different way of making war, different standards. The decapitation, though horrible and unnecessary, ranked small against some things he had witnessed.

In the last town, some of the ex-imperialists had caught a Juarista official. They flopped him on the ground, tied ropes to his arms and legs, and fastened the bite ends to the saddles of four horses. Then they set about to literally draw and quarter the unfortunate bureaucrat. Brisa and three of his retainers had taken the daughter of a Juarista to amuse themselves with, then took turns throwing her back and forth through a fire until she collapsed and was consumed by the flames. Disgusting.

"Colonel," Sergeant Nally had complained to him following that incident, "them people ain't hardly more'n animals. I've seen Comanche with more consideration for their captives."

"I know, Sergeant. Yet, they are, at the least, our allies, and they do represent a fifth of our entire force."

"Lord, I never thought we'd be a hunnerd-fifty strong," the lean, lank noncom observed.

"Hill bandits, even turncoats like the imperialists, like to back a winner. Right now we seem to be the biggest winner around," Kilgore offered his opinion. "I'd watch them, though. You should. I do."

"Yes, sir. God A'mighty, how they love blood. Makes my skin crawl sometimes."

"Ummm. Part of the culture. Remember seeing those

tall round structures in the larger towns, the cities we left alone?"

"Yes, sir. Never gave 'em much thought."

"Those are bull rings. They got the practice from the Spanish. These folks put a man with a scrap of cloth and a sword on a sand arena inside there with a thousand-pound, thoroughly angry bull. Sort of like the Romans did the Christian martyrs. They call it sport. Also, our hill-bandit friends are more Indian than Spanish. Their ancestors used to cut the living, beating hearts out of people for a religious sacrifice."

"Shit! Beggin' the colonel's pardon, sir. We've got us a bunch of bar . . . bar . . . savages among us."

Over the days that followed, Kilgore often recalled that conversation. Sergeant Nally was right: barbarians at the gates. All under his command. And when would the barbarians decide that they should be giving the orders? A terrified shriek from behind him attracted Colonel Kilgore's attention.

From a balcony window a young woman hung suspended by her hair. Two of the imperialists held hands full of her long black tresses. Lascivious grins illuminated their faces. Small feet flailed the air and her fingers reached desperately for a bougainvillea vine that climbed the wall.

"Estoy listo," one of them said.

The other nodded; he was ready also. *"Adiós, puta de los Juaristas."*

They let go.

"Good God!" Kilgore blurted.

Such a short fall did not kill her outright, the colonel discovered. Both of her legs were broken, and she no doubt suffered internal injuries, yet she breathed raggedly, a trickle of blood running from her mouth. Yes, Colonel Kilgore decided, something would definitely have to be done to curb their sadistic appetites.

Under a high noon sun, Canyon O'Grady and Carlos O'Marra sat munching cold beans rolled in tortillas, the leavings of a breakfast O'Marra had cooked. So far O'Grady had not detected any indication of pursuit. Small wonder when the ravaged town of Sabinas could hardly produce a half-dozen adult males.

"Mumph," O'Marra said around a mouthful of frijoles.

"I've been givin' it some thought. You may want to know
that I'll be riding along only until we reach the high road
for Torreón. Then I'll be goin' west."

Relieved, O'Grady started to frame a response that would
not sound ungrateful for all O'Marra had done for him so
far. His words died in his chest, his good intentions jolted
by his companion's next remark.

"Bein' a man of peace, I'd not be much good in an
encounter with those renegade soldiers."

"I told you last night that I wasn't . . ." O'Grady fought
for a convincing denial and found none. He tried to change
the topic. "What's it like in Torreón?"

"Peaceful, like I said. The right sort of place for me.
You, too, if I didn't reckon that you are hell-bent on a
showdown with Colonel Death."

Vultures circled in the sun-scorched air above the medi-
um-size town of Castaños, Coahuila. *Zopilotes* in Spanish,
Canyon O'Grady recalled. The trail of destruction led him
onward. He could read the unwelcome information that
their numbers must be growing in the increasing size of the
communities that fell victim to the army of looters.

Instead of attrition simplifying his job, O'Grady now realized that each passing day made it more difficult for him to
end the bloody career of Colonel Kilgore, Colonel Death.
The Mexican journalists had aptly named him. The damage
to Castaños was old, that much he could tell from a
distance.

In the last undamaged town, O'Grady had acquired more
traditional Mexican clothing. He now wore an embroidered
yellow shirt, which he considered somewhat frilly, a short
cut-off jacket of rust brown, matching skintight trousers
with big silver conchas along the outer seams, and a conser-
vative-size sombrero of the same color, picked out with a
silver thread. At least his appearance wouldn't immediately
betray him. In his business, one had to adapt.

Satisfied with that, Canyon O'Grady gigged Cormac with
his spurs and the stout palomino worked up to a gentle lope.
Mounted on twin pyramids of adobe blocks, a wrought-iron
fretwork screen formed an arch over the place where the
high road became a city street. A few bullet holes pockmarked the white plastered walls of houses nearest the town
limits. Further on, little overt damage could be seen.

O'Grady began to have hope that perhaps Kilgore's outlaw army had bitten off more than . . . No.

Ahead now he saw what must have been the business district, at least the central plaza and marketplace for Castaños. It was now a burned-out ruin. A few people moved about, women with the ubiquitous black rebozos over their heads and masking the lower halves of their faces, barefoot children with haunted eyes, old men, unshaven and gaunt. Nowhere did he see a man in the prime of life.

"Hola," one aged male greeted him. "Have you come from the army?"

"Lo siento, no, señor," O'Grady replied. In that moment he was truly sorry he had not come from the Mexican Army to bring relief for these people.

Disappointment flashed briefly in the old man's eyes. He sighed and worked his toothless mouth. "They never come, except to take, like the scum who did this." He gestured to the collapsed buildings, the blackened fire scars, empty window frames. "But . . ." He sighed. *"Todavia me tienes vivito y coleando."*

It took O'Grady a moment to make sense of the old-timer's philosophy. *Still alive and kicking.* What a sorry world when that's all one could say about his life and future. Damn Kilgore and his horde. O'Grady bade the old man farewell and continued across the plaza. From ahead of him he heard a faint sound, a sort of mewing, wailing cry. He approached the church and heard it more clearly.

Following an instinct, O'Grady tied off Cormac to a ring in a stone pillar and walked around the side of the burned-out house of worship. Behind was the *camposanto*, the cemetery. Fresh mounds of earth told the story of Castaños. By one, a black-garbed figure knelt, bent double with the force of grief, hands to face. From it came the anguished sounds. O'Grady walked closer. His foot crunched a clod against the cobbles of the path. The mourner stiffened, then turned around.

"Oh, thank God. You came, you really came," she said breathlessly.

O'Grady stared at a lovely young woman he had never before seen in his life. She rose gracefully and flung herself into his arms.

9

O'Grady stood with his arms awkwardly around the young lady he did not know. She pressed her face to his chest and sobbed unrestrainedly. He became acutely conscious of the warm, firm pressure of her breasts against his chest and wondered at grief so absolute that it permitted such intimacies with a total stranger. Gradually the crying subsided. She made a last hiccuping sob and raised her face.

"Oh, Miguel, I was so-oooo . . ." The color drained from her face and her lovely bright amber eyes went wide. "Y-you're not Miguel."

"No, miss. Canyon O'Grady at your service. I'm sorry to have intruded on your grief under what must appear to be false pretenses." By God, he'd managed all that in Spanish rather well. He *was* learning.

She broke free of his arms but did not retreat. "The error was all mine, Señor O'Grady. I thought you were my cousin Miguel Fernández. You look so like him in height and build, your clothes."

O'Grady removed his hat and received another surprised reaction from the remarkably lovely young woman. A titter of laughter burst from her full, sensuous lips. Immediately she covered her indiscretion with a small, well-shaped hand.

"That hair. Had you not been wearing a sombrero, I would have known at once. Forgive me. Doña Mercedes Elena Fernández y Obregón at your service, sir."

"May I settle for Mercedes?" O'Grady asked ingenuously.

"Of course, and your given name?"

"Canyon. My—ah—mother . . ." he began the accustomed explanation.

"I think it's lovely. So we shall be Mercedes and Canyon. *Que bueno*."

"It is apparent that the one called Coronel Muerte has

visited Castaños, but may I be permitted to inquire into the cause of your personal grief?"

For a moment Mercedes' eyes clouded and filled with tears. She blinked them back and gestured to three fresh graves. "My father and two older brothers. They were brutally murdered on orders from Coronel Muerte." She spat the name as if it were a mouthful of filth.

"I . . . am sorry. At a time of so much evil, it's difficult to see individual tragedies. I gather from the way you said it, they were singled out for some particular purpose?"

"Yes. Ah—let's stroll back toward the plaza. I have spent myself in weeping here. The soil in the *Camposanto* is well-watered by the survivors." She drew a deep breath, sighed it partly out as they walked. "Neither my father nor my brothers would reveal the location of our family valuables. Father has . . . *had* a strongbox hidden under the floor of his study. When those *ladrónes* found little of value in so large a house, your Colonel Death had my father dragged out into the patio. There we were forced to look on while the colonel's men tortured him."

"I gather he did not reveal the hiding place?" O'Grady prompted.

"He did not. Nor did Ramón when—after Father gave up his spirit. Ramón was very brave. He was young and healthy and so it took ever so long. I fainted. Several times, in fact. Th-then it was Jorge's turn. Stubborn like Ramón, he clung to life and defied the *bastardos gringos*. Oh!" Mercedes uttered a squeak and covered her mouth. "You are a *norteño* also, Canyon."

"I am, but not like them."

Somewhere during their conversation they had slipped from Spanish into English without noticing it. Mercedes spoke excellent English, O'Grady noted with pleasure. In fact, he enjoyed very much being with her. The circumstances dimmed it only a little. Under the mourner's weeds, he speculated, there must be a delightful body. He had sensed pleasing curves and those firm small breasts when she had sobbed on his shoulder. Keeping company with Mercedes Fernández was far from an onerous task. She laid a hand on his arm.

"I know that you're not. Somehow I sense something . . . noble about you. You are here for a purpose, aren't you, Canyon?"

There was no secret now about what Kilgore had been doing, O'Grady reasoned, so why evade the question? Especially when it came from so entrancing a young lady. "Yes, I am. I have been—ah—engaged to track down this man they call Colonel Death." He needn't tell all the truth, O'Grady reminded himself.

"You wear those clothes like a born *hidalgo*, and your Spanish, while not perfect, is passable. Let me guess. You have been sent by the government."

"Umm, yes. The government."

"Perhaps by Don Benito himself?"

"Ah—no. I don't even know the President of Mexico."

"*Más o menos, no importa*. It makes little difference," she repeated in English idiom. "You have come to avenge us all against that *monstruo*. I am content with that. When my *primo* Miguel arrives, we shall accompany you and exact our own retribution on Colonel Death for the lives of our family."

She said it with such vehemence that it set O'Grady back. For a moment he could make no reply. "I—ah—mine is a—ah—secret mission. I can't have a lot of people, especially untrained civilians, dragging along. You could . . . could be killed at any moment."

Mercedes' eyes flashed. "I am the last survivor. If I die avenging my family, at least my soul can be at rest."

She speaks like a character in a melodrama, O'Grady thought distractedly. "The point is, Mercedes, you are a young woman, a—ah—beautiful young woman. Your upbringing surely could not have prepared you for fighting bandits."

"My father taught me to ride and to shoot. Primo Miguel was my constant companion in childhood. He taught me many other things, including how to use a knife and fight with my fists."

"Not the usual education for a little girl," O'Grady opined. "Yet it hardly prepares you for the realities of what you would have to face in any conflict with Kil—uh—Colonel Death."

"You forget, Canyon, I have already seen the worst he can do. You have only encountered the aftermath," Mercedes responded heatedly. "I agree to this, let it wait until Miguel arrives. When he has come, we can make a final decision about it."

Grudging the point, O'Grady agreed.

* * *

Over the next two days, Mercedes effortlessly shed her grief, in a manner typically Latin and characteristic of youth. She did visit the graves of her family and wore a black mantilla and veil, though she had exchanged her somber dress for more colorful apparel. She began to aid O'Grady in his mastery of Spanish, particularly the reading and writing of the language. News of atrocities by Kilgore's private army dwindled, then ceased.

"They have reached the Sierra Madre," Mercedes stated confidently. "The mountains are vast and secretive. We will have to search them out."

Her determination to accompany O'Grady had not diminished. She spoke encouragingly of her cousin. Miguel Fernández took on grandly noble proportions. O'Grady suspected her of a secret childhood crush.

"He treated me like another of the boys," she told O'Grady at a late supper one night. "On my father's rancho outside of town we rode and went fishing, had hay fights, we even . . . even went swimming in the irrigation ponds with some of the sons of my father's workers. Oh, I know it was immodest, perhaps even sinful, but such great fun. Besides, once we got in the water up to our waists in one of the shallow *tanques*, we all looked alike."

"Have you seen much of Miguel lately?" O'Grady asked.

A frown creased Mercedes' sooth, high brow. Her crystal amber eyes, set below thin but vivid brows, narrowed. "No. Not since the fighting began against the imperialists. Miguel is a year and a half older than I, which makes him twenty-three. He fought bravely with the Juarista army. It has been . . . two years. And now he should be here soon." She brightened at the thought.

Midmorning of the next day brought a tall, thin, handsome young man to the gate of the town house. He wore his clothes with an accustomed casualness that stood out sharply compared to O'Grady's style. His broad white smile seemed to illuminate the day. Upon being admitted, he at once called loudly for Mercedes, arms spread wide. Mercedes rushed to him and jumped into his embrace, her hands behind his neck.

"Oh, Miguel, Miguel. I am so glad you are here." She recovered from her exuberance and spoke with slight reserve. "Set me down, Miguel. There is someone in the patio I want you to meet."

When Miguel Fernández saw the tall, thick-shouldered gringo with the flame hair, he raised thin aristocratic brows of the same ebon hue as Mercedes' and tilted his chin so he looked somewhat down a long, straight nose at the visitor. Mercedes made the introductions and explained that O'Grady had been her protector since the majority of the servants had been killed or run off.

"I am grateful, Señor O'Grady. You are a countryman of ours?" he inquired, sizing up O'Grady's clothing.

"No. I am from the United States," he took the plunge.

Miguel's eyes narrowed again. "Your government took an unusually long time to recognize the government of Presidente Juárez," he observed.

"Not my doing," O'Grady stated simply.

"But Canyon is here to do something about those *ladrónes*," Mercedes injected by way of peacemaking.

"Oh? Is that so? And what do you propose to do with the army of Colonel Death?" Miguel asked with a slight note of irritation in his voice.

"As little as possible," O'Grady responded, suddenly finding his plan coalesced in his head. "I intend to remove Colonel Death—his name is Kilgore—and any of the men who deserted with him that I can capture. With the head cut off, his so-called army will dissolve quickly."

To O'Grady's surprise, Miguel nodded in approval. "An ambitious undertaking, but not impossible, I think. How many men are with you?"

O'Grady produced a wry smile. "I am alone."

"*¡Madre de Dios!* It's no small thing you wish to do." Miguel began to pace the patio. "You must have help. That much is obvious. I can raise twenty-five, perhaps thirty men."

"Who will flounder around in the mountains and either warn Kilgore away or provoke a pitched battle," O'Grady rejected. "I will have to do it alone."

"Permit me to offer myself and a few good men. I must. It is my duty to Mexico," Miguel protested hotly.

"And *I* am going," Mercedes injected.

Miguel looked at her as though she had gone mad. "That, my little *prima*, you are not doing."

"I've tried to tell her that," O'Grady began. "It has had little effect."

Hands on hips, Mercedes stamped one foot. "I am going. I have my duty too, Miguel."

"Out of the question. It is too dangerous."

"I can shoot. I can ride a horse. I can cook too," Mercedes insisted.

Miguel made a face. "I remember sampling some of your cooking. Better we take old Tía Juanita. Now, she can cook. Which reminds me, it is nearing time for the *almuerzo*. I am aching with hunger."

"How can you talk of food when there is our revenge to plan?" Checked by the expressions on the faces of O'Grady and Miguel, she moderated her stand. "Lunch will be served at the usual time. Until then, why don't you and Canyon talk of how you can capture or kill this Colonel Kilgore?"

"A good idea, *mija*. We shall do that," Miguel said heartily.

For the balance of the day, O'Grady and Fernández discussed possible means by which Colonel Kilgore could be apprehended and removed from Mexico. O'Grady saw the advantage of having fighting men to back his move when he made it, if for no other reason than to have a rear guard to delay pursuit once the mad colonel had been captured. In the end, they agreed that Miguel would visit Mercedes' father's rancho and return with a dozen good men. They would be picked from among those who had soldiered with the army of Benito Juárez and knew the intricacies of combat. Mercedes' "outside town" turned out to be a full day's journey to the west. Miguel would take several days to complete the task. He spent the night at the town house and departed early in the morning.

Through the day, Mercedes put on her most winning smiles. She proved agreeable in everything, except one subject. She remained adamant that she would accompany the search for Kilgore. Bit by bit, her light banter and innuendo took on a coloration of romantic interest. Not that Canyon O'Grady minded. She was lovely to look at, and older than he had estimated.

Her lively amber eyes reminded him of a cat his mother had considered a favorite. She moved with near-feline grace also. She was small in general proportions, but her mouth widened intriguingly when she smiled. Which was something Mercedes did a great deal more of during the long day. She issued an invitation to a late supper, the two of them on the patio of the damaged-but-serviceable town house. The idea appealed. O'Grady accepted with a mounting eagerness.

"At nineteen hours, then?" Mercedes asked. "We can sample one of my father's rare wines and watch the sun set."

"Sure sounds delightful," O'Grady agreed.

When the appointed hour came, O'Grady appeared at the now-repaired wrought-iron gate, dressed in Mexican finery. An old man showed him through the outer yard and to the other gate that barred entrance to the house. There he bowed low and made a broad gesture with one arm, indicating the passage through to the patio.

"The *señorita* is awaiting you on the patio, *señor*."

"*Gracias.*"

Mercedes was a vision of beauty, dressed gaily for the first time since Canyon O'Grady had seen her in the graveyard. She greeted him warmly, grasped both his hands, and rose on tiptoe to kiss him lightly on one cheek. Chattering brightly, she led him to a stairwell and upward to the landing. A private dining room with French doors on both sides gave access to an outward-facing balcony.

A marble-topped wrought-iron table had been spread with *entremeses* of a wide variety. There was a fruit plate, tiny tamales, a large plate of nachos, fish-and-cheese-stuffed chile peppers, and a chafing dish steaming with the savory aroma of roast breast of turtle. A napkin-wrapped bottle of wine and two glasses waited on another table. The sun, a rich orange, hung a hand's breadth above the rolling sandhills to the west. Shades of magenta tinged the fiery ball as O'Grady poured wine and they touched rims in salute.

" 'A loaf of bread, a jug of wine, and thou beside me in the wilderness,' " O'Grady quoted, a playful smile quirking his lips.

"One of your Irish poets, Canyon?" Mercedes asked.

"No. Omar Khayam. A poet of far-off Araby, Persian actually. When my father sent me back to the Auld Sod to acquire a well-rounded education, the good fathers at the priory gave me a far more eclectic study of the classics than old Dad expected."

"It sounds . . . romantic."

"It is. A scandalous poem of salacious images and wanton desires," he teased. He sampled a tuna-stuffed chile. "Umm. This is good," he managed from a burning mouth. "Different, but good."

"Blistering hot, you mean. Take some wine, then try a little fruit," Mercedes prescribed.

They finished the bottle of wine while the sun stole away, to be replaced by a diamond dusting of stars by the time their supper was announced. Again Mercedes led the way to the flagstoned patio. A table had been laid and gleamed with silver, snowy linen, and a five-stick candelabrum. O'Grady held the chair for Mercedes, then took his own place.

For all their nibbling, O'Grady found himself growing hungry. More so when the unfamiliar plate piled high with cubes of crisp-edged pork, a platter of assorted condiments, and a wicker basket of fresh-made tortillas came to their table. Small dishes of rice and beans appeared at their elbows.

"*Carnitas.* Delicious," Mercedes explained the meat dish. "Here, this is the way you eat them."

O'Grady watched her build a custom soft taco out of the meat and chopped vegetables. He followed suit and bit into a savory delight unlike anything he had eaten before. Not ordinarily a trencherman, O'Grady knew a good thing when he came on it. He chewed and nodded his head, his whole face alight with the pleasure he took in the blending of flavors.

"You see!" Mercedes cried happily. "I'll make a *mejicano* out of you yet."

A look passed between them, fleeting, yet powerful in its message. O'Grady felt a familiar stirring. A crackling sexual tension grew in the space between their faces, bright and rosy in the candlelight. O'Grady cleared his mouth with a swallow of wine.

" 'In the scented bud of the morning—O,' " he quoted. " 'When the windy grass went rippling far/ I saw my dear one walking slow/ In the field where the daisies are. We did not laugh and we did not speak/ As we wandered happily to and fro/ I kissed my dear on either cheek/ In the bud of the morning—O.' You've never been quite so beautiful as tonight," he said softly.

"Was that an Irish poem?" she asked, made nervous by the fervor in his voice.

"Yes. It's called *The Daisies*."

Still upset, Mercedes lowered her lashes. "It's not proper . . . what I am doing, with Father hardly cold in his grave. I should not be gay and laughing."

"And why not?" O'Grady asked in Gaelic dudgeon. "With we Irish, it's all done and over with after the wake. You're a young lass, and a quite pulchritudinous one I might add, and you've so much of your life ahead of you. Tragedies happen. When they are past, it's time to move on. Trust me in that."

"Do you really think so? That I am attractive?"

"You're—you're . . . splendorous. 'Age cannot wither, nor custom stale her infinite variety. Other women cloy the appetites they feed, while she makes hungry where most she satisfies.' That's from the Bard of Avon."

O'Grady took one small hand, held it like a captive bird. "Mercedes, Mercedes, you have a power over me, perhaps over all men—I saw how you make Miguel come alive, and he's your cousin—that defies words. I can't describe it, only . . . demonstrate."

"The poem is lovely." Mercedes evaded the subject, fighting her own swelling attraction.

"There's more. 'A lark sang up from the breezy land/ A lark sang down from a cloud afar/ And she and I went hand in hand/ In the field where the daisies are.' "

"Oh, Canyon, take me where the daisies are. Take me upstairs. To my room. I'll show you the way."

Hand in hand they climbed the stairs. Mercedes made tiny, rapid footsteps down the roofed-over inner balcony. At one large carved door she stopped. A winsome smile curved her lips. O'Grady started to speak, and she pressed a finger against his lips. Her hand found the latch and, with a tug, she drew him inside.

They kissed beyond the door. Mercedes rose on tiptoe, arms twined around Canyon's neck. He embraced her tightly, shivering at the pleasant sensation of her small firm breasts against his chest. Not even the layers of cloth could rob the contact of excitement. Her mouth opened and a moan came as he probed avidly with his tongue. After long minutes the kiss ended.

Only to begin again. Her dress proved a torture to loosen

and remove. They worked at it together, baffled by its intri-
cacy. At last the lacings and buttons yielded. Trembling
with suppressed passion, Mercedes thrilled to the feel of his
hands exploring her bare shoulders, the hard globes of her
breasts. His thumbs set her trembling as they massaged the
swollen nipples. She gasped as he ranged downward and
plucked at the drawstring of her many petticoats. Eager,
yet fearful, for him to continue, she fumbled at the buttons
of his shirt. He had shed his jacket.

Mercedes pulled his shirttails free of the trousers and he
shrugged out of it. "Hold me, oh, hold me again, Canyon,"
she pleaded.

A shock ran through both as their bare flesh made tight
contact from shoulder to waist. Fully aroused, Canyon's
rampant manhood strained against his trousers. Conscious
of its pressure, Mercedes instinctively ground her pubic
mound against it. Hot and sweet, she sensed her flowing
juices. Her hands found his belt buckle, loosened it. The
fly buttons leapt from their place. A soft whisper and her
petticoats came away to flutter down around her ankles.

Her swift though inexperienced movements had Canyon
out of his trousers. They hung from his boot tops. Only
then did either of them think of their footwear.

"Oh, my," Mercedes squeaked. "We can't—can't do anything until our feet are free."

O'Grady began a low, throaty laugh. "We've a sayin'
about a cart and a horse, my dear, dear lass. Never you
mind. We'll be out of these things in no time."

"I hope so, oh, I so hope we will," Mercedes pleaded.

O'Grady performed the necessary functions with skill and
ease. Then he scooped Mercedes from her feet and carried
her to the bed. A tall satin-canopied tester bed, it had
ample room for two. She quaked now with ardor and over-
stimulation. O'Grady frowned.

"Is it afraid you are?" he asked.

"No—no. Not of you. I could never be afraid of you.
Hurry, Canyon, make me truly come alive again."

He laid her gently on her back and crawled in next to
her, to rest on one side. O'Grady began to explore her
every nook, curve, and plane with sensitive fingers and lips.
Little whimpers came from Mercedes as he increased the
intensity of his foreplay. His own state of excitement had

him vibrating with the effort to hold back. Eventually it was Mercedes who could endure no more.

"Take me, Canyon. Oh, hurry, beloved. Take me."

O'Grady roused himself and slid sensuously between her creamy thighs. She writhed with overwhelming excitement. When he had positioned himself, she pressed a tiny hand against his chest.

"Be gentle, *amado*. I—it—this is only my s-second time."

"Extraordinary," Canyon croaked.

"It is. I hid from the looters. They never found me or I would have been ruined like so many others. There has truly been only once. When I was fourteen. A friend of Miguel's. He was—umm—two years older. We were both mad with desire. We weakened. It was . . . enjoyable, exciting, if not completely satisfactory. I have remained constant since. Now—now I want to surrender all to you, dearest Canyon."

Touched, moved almost to a whimsical mood, O'Grady exercised the patience and forbearance of Job. Ever so slowly he entered her. He found her hot, wet, and ready. The penetration progressed in tiny increments. With each minute lunge, Mercedes cried out in an ecstasy that transcended any pain. By the time O'Grady hilted himself and felt the wondrous pressure of their pubic arches grinding together, they both became dizzy with unbridled passion.

After a long pause he extracted his throbbing member, to plunge again, and again. In measured pace he increased the frequency of each thrust. Mercedes groaned and hugged him tightly. Their beings blended, merged, dissolved, and spun joyfully away until the moment of oblivion, which gave them such frenzied release that they lay stunned, unable to disengage or even to move.

It would be, O'Grady promised them both silently, only the first of many ecstatic encounters on that night. Ruefully he realized that Mercedes had also made her point, leaving him breathless and eager to have some companionship on the trail after Kilgore.

10

When two more days passed and Miguel had not returned, Canyon O'Grady decided to start on his own. Mercedes would accompany him. At least, he decreed, until the situation reached a point of real danger. She had shared his bed since the night of her dinner party. He soon found she had a healthy, amorous spirit and an eagerness to learn. It tried all of O'Grady's skills to patiently instruct her in the many ways of love. Mercedes proved an apt pupil. With all preparations made the night before, the morning of their departure dawned to lowering clouds and a storm-charged atmosphere. Regardless, O'Grady determined to push on.

They left word for Miguel that they were headed for Reata in the state of Nuevo León. A new spate of reports on plundered villages directed them into the mountains to the east of the small community. Miguel could follow easily from that point. Moist air from the Gulf of Mexico collided with the storm front and brought a heavy downpour to Castaños as they left the city behind.

"We're well out of that," O'Grady observed, glancing back at the charcoal curtains of rain that descended on Castaños.

"Where will we spend the night, *amado*?" Mercedes asked, always the practical one.

"Somewhere on the trail, I imagine," O'Grady told her. He felt good, warm and glowing from wonderful loving. Head thrown back, he opened his mouth in song, his voice a clear, pure tenor.

> O Paddy dear! an' did ye hear,
> the news that's goin' round?
> The shamrock is forbid by law,
> to grow on Irish ground.
> No more St. Patrick's Day we'll keep;

> his color can't be seen.
> For there's a cruel law ag'in',
> the Wearin' o' the Green.

Abruptly he stopped. "Ah, that's too sad for such a day. How about this?"

> Sure I love the dear silver,
> that shines in her hair.
> And I love her dear fingers,
> so toil-worn with care.
> O! I love her sweat prayers,
> she oft gave up for me.
> O! God bless you and keep you,
> Mother McCree.

Mercedes laughed delightedly. "Every day you manage to amaze me with something new, Canyon. Oh, what fun it is to be with you. I . . . I only wish we were set upon a happier course than the one we're pursuing."

"Now, now, Mercy-lass. This is not a time for sorrow or regrets. All will work itself out in due time." O'Grady sincerely hoped his prediction proved true.

All too soon their light mood deserted them. O'Grady's sensitive nostrils picked up the odor long before Mercedes realized anything was amiss. A flock of mixed carrion birds hovered over the crumbled remains of a village. Rotting corpses greeted the travelers as they entered the scene of ruin. Mercedes gagged and turned away, covering her mouth.

"Canyon—*Dios mío*, this is terrible. How can anyone be so savage, so merciless?"

"Maybe now you understand better why I want to keep you away from the fighting when and if it begins," he told her quietly.

She only nodded. "We must—must do something for all these poor people."

"What, Mercedes? We haven't time, energy, or space to bury them all."

His harsh tone, born of revulsion and regret, might have been a slap in the face. Mercedes recoiled from his heated words and widened her eyes as though suddenly encountering a stranger. "At least . . . we must pray for them."

"Do so, then," he snapped, damning himself for overreacting.

Mercedes made the sign of the cross and prayed silently for several minutes. Sighing, she wiped a tear from her cheek and faced O'Grady again.

"I am ready. Let's go on."

At the next village they encountered some twenty-five sorry survivors. At first the wretches ran and hid from them, until Mercedes called out that they meant no harm and had food for the hungry. Despite the urgency gnawing at him, O'Grady decided to spend the night there. Mercedes rewarded his announcement with a beaming smile so warm it stirred him to his loins.

After a supper of beans and fried ham, the first petitioner came to them. A grizzled old man, he held an ancient flintlock rifle in one gnarled hand. Whipping his straw sombrero from his head, he placed it over his heart and executed a curt bow to O'Grady.

"*Patrón*, I have come—ah—we of the village—I have been sent to—to ask you to accept us as your retainers. We wish to be taken along."

"I am going after the man responsible for what was done to your village and many more," O'Grady stated coldly. "Why would you want to accompany me?"

Puzzlement washed over the old-timer's face. "Why, to avenge our wives, daughters, sons, and parents. We are not many, those able to fight, but we have great resolve, *patrón*."

"I'm sure you do, *viejo*. Unfortunately, stout hearts can come in frail bodies, or those too young to sacrifice in a battle."

"Oh, no, no, *patrón*," a clear, high voice contradicted from outside the roofless house in which O'Grady sat with Mercedes. A boy entered, not more than fourteen years in age, yet with an aged bulky .44 Colt Dragoon pistol jammed in the waistband of his white cotton trousers. "We are not too old, or too young. We must do our duty to our families. Please, *patrón*, let us come with you."

Other voices joined his. O'Grady rose, the kerosene lantern they had brought along held high in one hand, and walked outside. He counted some seventeen persons, many who had not been seen before. They all had weapons of one sort or another, mostly ancient and discolored with rust.

"A fine lot you are," he growled, trying to put scorn into his words, though his heart swelled with admiration for such raw courage. "How far do you think you could get?"

"Far enough, *patrón*, to hang that *cabrón* and all his scum," a brave voice called. The man stepped forward. "I may have only one arm, but with it I can haul on the end of a rope. I can shoot too. I gave my arm for Benito Juárez and freedom. I'll not let this bandit filth turn my sacrifice into *mierda*."

A tightness bound O'Grady's throat. This reminded him of his grandfather's tales of the Uprising. Of Brendan on the Moor, and brave deeds done in the name of Ireland and the Holy Faith. These were the stuff of which heroes were made. He wanted to curse them, to tell them to leave him alone, but his Irish heart wept for them and sang praises to their courage.

"A-all right, lads, all right," he managed at last. "There's some men coming along behind us. They are led by Miguel Fernández, late of the army of Benito Juárez. Eat the food we left you, rest, and grow stronger. When they arrive, those of you who are truly fit may join him. And God bless you, each and every one."

More deeply moved than at any time since that great and noble man Abraham Lincoln had been assassinated, Canyon O'Grady turned away and went back inside with Mercedes. He hadn't time to collect his emotions, for she leapt upon him, raining hugs and kisses.

"Oh, lover, your skin is that of a gringo, but your heart is Mexican."

"My gringo skin and my heart haven't anything to do with it, m'love. 'Tis the soul of an Irishman you've seen tonight."

Afterward, when they had disentangled and the lights had been extinguished, they made long, slow, utterly fantastic love until the stars tilted sideways in heaven.

"Here it is." Colonel Judson Kilgore breathed deeply, savoring the thin, biting air of the high mountains. "The Sierra Madre Oriental—the Eastern Mother Mountains. A man could count himself rich just to live here in peace and comfort."

"Getting tired of—ah—'campaigning,' Jud?" Captain Lancelot Means asked with an edge in his voice.

Kilgore turned in the saddle. "What do you mean, Lance?"

"Nothing, nothing. Only the men are tired, the horses are beat to hell, and we're short on rations. Ammunition, too. You know, I've just found out that a lot of these bandidos who have joined us actually believe that it is the noise that makes a man fall down, not the bullet. They don't even aim. With allies like that, we could exhaust our ammo supply damn fast."

"What do you propose?" Kilgore asked, watching his tactical officer closely.

"There's no sign of pursuit. We're clear the hell and gone in these mountains, and we've the money to buy some necessary supplies. I feel it's time to call a halt for a while. Find someplace and hole up until we recover our prime fighting ability. And there's the wounded to consider."

"Agreed. I've been thinking the same for a while. It's our good fortune that the scouts told me of a place last night. Not far from here, and ideal for our needs." Kilgore's voice took on a note of cynicism. "Even the name fits our enterprise: Villadolor—the Village of Sorrow."

"What's it like?" Means inquired.

"According to Navarro and Gordon, it's built like a medieval town in Europe, with a high stone wall surrounding the whole place. Inside that the outer walls of the buildings form another wall. There are gates, strong ones, and parapets along the outer wall. The defenses even include three round flat-topped towers along one side that mount little six-pounder cannon. Together they command the entire trail through the pass that Villadolor overlooks."

"Sounds tough. How do you propose to take the place?"

"Simple. We send in our Mexican auxiliaries—the bandits—first, then the imperialists, a few at a time. Then . . ."

"Cuatro días, patrón," the squat, toothless man with once-black hair fading to mouse-tone informed Canyon O'Grady.

"Four days," O'Grady repeated aloud in English.

By hard riding they had closed the gap. Still no sign of Miguel and the dozen vaqueros he had promised. Where did that leave him? In a deep pile, no question of that. All his plans had been laid on the basis of a rear guard to delay, misdirect, and confuse any pursuit by Kilgore's loyal troops.

Now he and Mercedes stood in the ruins of yet another village, the bedraggled people of the community gathered around them. O'Grady had to admit to himself he hadn't any sort of plan on how to deal with Kilgore alone. The strategy hatched with Miguel depended on the fact that Kilgore would not know O'Grady, nor Miguel, could not, having never seen either of them. They would pick a time and a place, join in with the outlaw band, and when opportunity presented, spirit Kilgore away in the middle of the night.

He held his trepidations in check until they cleared the village. Once more those few physically able to seriously consider revenge begged to come along. Again he left the same offer. When Miguel Fernández arrived, they could join him. He also left word for Miguel that they would take the right-hand trail out of Ciudad Malchor. It headed for the main pass through the Sierra Madre to Monterrey.

They made camp in the foothills, and while Mercedes prepared the evening meal, O'Grady broached the subject of a workable plan. After explaining what had been previously decided, he concluded with, "So now that might not be workable. Something may have happened to Miguel. I have to come up with something brilliant to solve the problem."

"I understand the difficulties a lot more now, *amado*." She smiled wistfully, as though giving up a cherished childhood belief. "I had intended to dress alluringly, let myself be seen by this Colonel Death, and make him desire me. Then, when I got up close, I would slip a knife between his ribs and finish the pig right there."

"How about getting away?"

She gave O'Grady a speculative look. "You know, I hadn't considered that."

They lapsed into silence, which held through the meal, each consumed in the complexities of finding a plan that would work. When the last tin plate and cup had been rinsed in a chill mountain stream, Mercedes came and sat beside O'Grady on a large boulder, still warm from the afternoon sun.

"Now what?" she asked glumly.

"Now, my wonderful lass, I am going to make love to you and for you in such a manner that you will never be able to frown again."

Mercedes tittered. "You can think of that when we are no closer to a way to end Colonel Kilgore?"

"I can think of *that* anytime, *mecushla*. Especially around you."

"Then show me," she taunted. "Show me right now."

Her peal of laughter cut off in a gasp of surprise when O'Grady peeled out of his shirt in one easy, fluid motion. His boots clunked against the granite formation on which they sat. In no time his trousers joined the boots. With a deft flick of his wrist, her flat-crown Cordoban sombrero went sailing.

"Oh, Canyon, oh!" she squeaked.

The front of his half-pair of long johns gave evidence of his amorous intentions. Mercedes stared at the risen bulge with fascination. Her fingers fumbled at the buttons of her riding-habit shirt. The split-front skirt came next. She wore a shiftlike garment that covered her from below her small pert breasts to mid-thigh. Canyon O'Grady went after the tie-string with avid digits. Her hand flew to his waist.

Drawstrings raced each other. O'Grady came up a winner, and her filmy garment floated gracefully to the ground. His underdrawers quickly followed. Mercedes looked around at the smoothed surface of the rock, the big swollen moon above, tips of swaying pines. Somewhere an owl hooted.

"Here?" she asked in consternation. "You mean we're going to do it right here?"

"Why not? I—ah—brought a blanket."

"All men are beasts, plotters, and schemers," she spat in mock disgust. "Here I am about to be sacrificed like some—some vir—*Ay!* I'm certainly not that. Not anymore. Thanks to you, my beloved, I am completely deflowered, degraded, and decidedly happy about it."

"And I about you. Now, be a good girl and help get these off from around my ankles. I can't chase you and subdue you in the proper manner with cotton legirons confining me."

"Helpless, eh? I've got you where I want you." Advancing, Mercedes knelt before the man she dreamed of, awake as well as asleep. Her hands started for his ankles, then halted, veered to close in on another object. Gently she encircled his swollen member and began to stroke it.

"Aaah, my dear, you have the perfect instinct for any given moment. Nothing could please me more . . . for now."

"Then I shall hurry on and be more inventive." Guided by instinct, she leaned forward and delivered a large, ripe, luscious kiss on the sensitive tip of his splendid manhood.

O'Grady shivered. He placed one hand lightly on the back of her head and urged her forward. Mercedes obliged, opening wide, eyes closed, like a child anticipating that first bite of ice cream. She closed silken lips over his pulsing lance and worked to accommodate its unaccustomed presence and bulk, then began to rock back and forth.

After several long ecstatic minutes, O'Grady spoke gently. "The drawers, love, get the drawers off my legs or I'm liable to pitch over the side and break something."

"Oh, not this, I pray," Mercedes gasped, releasing her suctioning hold on his phallus.

"Now, that would be a tragedy beyond any recovery. No, I was thinking of my neck. There, now, yes, good." He bent and lifted her to her feet.

Their lips met in a long, passionate kiss that grew in ardor with each passing second. Hands explored, bodies tingled, and the first faint heralds of what would come next sent shivers up their spines. Slowly they sank to their knees. O'Grady's big square hands eased Mercedes into a supine position.

He exercised superb tenderness when he placed himself between her open thighs. Fingers thickened by hard work sought out the sparsely thatched cleft which welcomed him gleefully. He probed, rotated, delved, stretched, then plunged his powerful shaft into the wetly prepared socket.

Mercedes squealed in delight. She rose to meet his thrust, arms encircling him, slender, shapely legs entrapping his body. His hips pistoned and each thrust brought new joys to them. Celestial lights flashed, a hidden chorus sang paeans of praise to Eros. The earth shivered, the stars fell, the moon faded to a dim coin in the sky. Alone with each other, they became one.

Time fled, minutes absorbed into a quarter-hour, that into half an hour. Mercedes cried out in fulfillment, O'Grady pressed on.

Undaunted, he strove to make this the very best. Nagging him was the knowledge that only four or so days separated him from Colonel Kilgore. At the next decent town he would have to leave Mercedes behind. He wanted her happy, remembering him and wanting him back terribly when they parted, and for long after. The magic held. Three-quarters of an hour had been spent in gradual, repeated approaches to the ultimate. Striving and restraining had to be paid for with cramps and twinges. Neither partner felt them as pain. Only pleasure filled their special night.

At last the flood could be contained no longer. With a mighty rush they ascended the pinnacle and burst in dazzling brightness over the brink into the minute oblivion that slowly, slowly ebbed.

"Nice," Mercedes murmured after a long return to reality. "Oh, so nice."

"Thank you, dear one, and thank you for making my night so perfect."

Slowly O'Grady disengaged himself. Instantly Mercedes reached for him. "Is that it? Don't tell me that's all you have energy for?"

"Oh, no. There can be much more. There *will* be. Only, I think we're a bit exposed up here. Let's go back to camp and make love to each other under the trees."

"Oh, yes, yes. Hurry. Gather our things and we'll run naked through the forest. You're so—so won-der-ful, Can-yon, so wooon-derrrr-fuuuul."

11

Thick dark gray bellies filled with water rose from the gulf plain. They grew in volume until they reached the sawtooth eastern peaks of the Sierra Madre Oriental. There they discharged a large portion of their content. Progressing westward, they gathered more moisture until they clashed with heated clouds bearing subtropical moisture, turmoil-generated by long passage across country from the Pacific and Sea of Cortez.

When this kink of nature occurred over the western slopes of the mountains, torrential downpours resulted. Swirling billows of charcoal gray had begun to build when Canyon O'Grady and Mercedes started out the next morning. Filled with the euphoria of their night of lovemaking, O'Grady had no hint of the potential they represented. Gradually the tall cumulonimbus formations grew in volume and thrust upward over thirty-eight thousand feet. Their anvil-headed upper reaches shone snowy bright in the sunlight. Mountain grouse and a variety of songbirds started up at their swift progress.

By midmorning their pace slowed markedly. Steep inclines greeted them as the ascent of the Sierra began. Above, unnoticed, nature prepared a drama of cataclysmic proportions. Intent on the trail and their surroundings, O'Grady caught his first indication of the pending uproar when the sun faded out under the approaching eastbound tempest behind them. He looked up and tingled with unease.

"Storm brewing," he observed to Mercedes. "Big one."

"Yes. This time of year there are violent ones in the Sierra."

"We had better look for someplace to shelter."

"It may be leagues to the next hacienda or a village."

O'Grady said nothing. He rode along with eyes carefully examining the terrain for any indication of a place to settle in before the downpour began. In half an hour they had found nothing. A loud roar from ahead jerked his attention to the maintained roadway they followed. In a fleeting moment his ears identified the sound.

A cascade of water bore down on them from beyond the next bend in the road. Somewhere in the higher reaches the clouds had released their store of moisture and formed a flash flood. To the right he saw a canyon opening that led away from the general area of the roiling billows of gray-black. Overhead the tumbling masses met. A sizzling bolt of lightning split the air less than five hundred yards away.

O'Grady heard it buzz and crackle an instant before an apocalyptic blast of thunder shook the ground. The air smelled of ozone. Cormac whuffled nervously and the other horses whinnied in fear. O'Grady pointed to the opening in the high granite walls.

"Over that way. We've got to get out of the way of that flood."

Sheets of rain washed over the land. Thumb-size drops stung exposed skin and soaked their clothes in seconds. At an awkward lope O'Grady and Mercedes started for the hoped-for shelter of the branch canyon.

Gasping from the combined effects of a rough ride and the storm, they reached the promised refuge a good two minutes before the avalanche of limbs, tree trunks, rocks, and foaming water boiled past the spot where they had halted on the road. The rain did not abate. O'Grady took stock of their situation.

"We keep going this way. Look for high ground, a ledge, a cave, someplace to take shelter."

"There are plenty of big trees," Mercedes suggested.

"No trees. They draw lightning," O'Grady rejected. For all it was too late, he untied his yellow India rubber slicker and donned it. Mercedes followed suit.

"It's getting worse," she observed.

"We keep moving for now."

Water began to rise in the creek that ran through the bottom of the southeast-slanted canyon. After fifteen minutes the rain had not slackened. Ahead, to the right, and slightly above them, O'Grady made out what appeared to be a darker smudge against the gray invisibility of the rain and low-scudding cloud wisps. Drawing closer, he became more convinced. He reined his palomino and peered into the tumult.

"Do you think you can get your horse to climb without dismounting?" he asked Mercedes in a shout over the howl of the wind.

"I—suppose so."

O'Grady pointed, indicating the dark presence in the storm. "Something up there. Could be shelter for us. Follow close behind me."

Cormac took the grade with ease for the first hundred feet. Slick mud checked the animal's advance. Chest muscles churning, he labored to make progress. A touch of rein and O'Grady dismounted. Blundering forward, he drew Cormac and the packhorse on up the slope. Biting her lip in worry, Mercedes followed. Another seventy-five feet and they gained a weathered ledge.

From this distance O'Grady could see that the black blob had been formed by a large overhang. Urging himself and the horses forward, he covered the distance in two slippery minutes. The cut extended well back into the hillside, offering dry ground. Someone had used the place as a temporary dwelling, O'Grady noted. A crude hitchrail had been constructed of debarked pine limbs. He tied off the horses and turned to help Mercedes.

She needed no assistance, he discovered. Her face furrowed with frown lines, she brought her sturdy mare in out of the rain. The animal promptly snorted in irritation and shook itself, showering them with drops of water.

"Tie her up," O'Grady prompted, "while I look for some firewood."

"Do you think . . . ?"

"Someone has used this place before. The tie-rail is evidence of that. And there's a fire ring over there."

In the back of the wedge-shaped defile, he located enough twigs and split lengths of pine to kindle a small blaze. Gratefully they warmed themselves, steam soon rising off their sodden clothing. O'Grady took a deep breath, pungent with pine resin, and thought of food.

"Looks like we'll be here a spell. Might as well fix a hot meal before the firewood runs out."

Alarm flashed on Mercedes' face. "Will it . . . ?"

"Soon," O'Grady assured her.

Three-quarters of an hour later they had beans ready, with reconstituted *machaca* and tortillas to make soft tacos. Sun-dried tomatoes, roasted chiles, and dry onions became *salsa*. O'Grady ate with gusto and considered the meal a resounding success. The fire had subsided to a low glow of coals. Beyond the lip of the overhang the rain continued.

"It could go on like this," Mercedes advised. "What do we do?"

"We wait," O'Grady answered.

Frequently O'Grady went to the edge to examine the water level on the floor of the canyon. It rose steadily. By nightfall it had covered half the distance to the ledge and O'Grady suspected these torrential storms had been responsible for the formation of the overhang. All amorous thoughts banished by the wet and cold, they huddled together for warmth. When the last glow of the fire faded, water lapped at the rim of the ledge.

During the night, a horse stamped in irritation, accompanied by a splash. O'Grady awakened to find the water swirling lazily past their boot heels. Much more and they would be lost.

Morning found the water down below the roadway. Good drainage left only a few potholes and stretches of slippery mud. While Mercedes made ready to continue the journey, O'Grady backtracked to the main thoroughfare through the mountains. He found the way blocked with a jumble of fallen trees, washed-out roadbed, at least one mudslide, and residual high water.

"We'll keep on this way," he announced when he returned. "At least it goes near to the right direction."

By noon they had climbed through a narrow pass, where an intermittent waterfall now cascaded voluminously to the creekbed below. Beyond the saddleback, they found a high plateau, rimmed by jagged peaks. Far in the distance, over the fertile valley, O'Grady thought he could make out wisps of smoke. Perhaps a village, he speculated. At least a large hacienda.

They advanced at a steady pace. In midafternoon the shapes of buildings could be discerned. Encouraged, O'Grady quickened their gait to a lope. Within twenty minutes they could make out details. It was a village, without a doubt. Yet such an odd one, considering the location. The structures had peaked roofs, clapboard sides, and the main street had been laid out along a wide tree-lined esplanade dividing its center. At the far end stood a whitewashed church. One intersection widened into a sort of square, with a bandstand, benches, and a big shade tree. In front of what must be the municipal center, two flagpoles rose into the sky, shiny brass balls topping each.

At the edge of town, after riding past neatly defined, well-tended fields on both sides of the road, a sign identified the community in bold letters:

LEESBERG
Población 357

Its incongruity arrested O'Grady's movement. He checked Cormac and stared at it, then at the buildings of the town. A vagrant puff of breeze lifted the lazily furled flags at the municipal center and extended them to clear view. One displayed the red, white, and green horizontal bars emblazoned with the eagle, cactus, and snake of the Mexican national emblem. The other had a vertical red bar on the flying edge, a white body with curled olive wreath, and three gold letters, CSA, and a blue field in the upper-left corner with the crossbar X and stars of the Confederacy.

"What in hell?" O'Grady blurted aloud.

He became aware of other things now. Barefoot, sun-browned, towheaded children gawked at him and Mercedes from the roadside. Men in the fields, though often bare to the waist, wore trousers of butternut or gray, with colored stripes down the outer seams. Along the main street, women strolled in crinolines with many petticoats, twirling parasols, their lace-trimmed bonnets bobbing as they walked.

Riding closer, O'Grady became aware that the styles were those of the late 1850s and early 60s. Antebellum finery. All the scene lacked was a passel of darky slaves fetching and carrying for the young ladies. Somehow a whole hamlet had been taken out of Virginia, North Carolina, or Georgia and plunked down wholesale in the mountains of Mexico. O'Grady spoke with wry assurance to Mercedes.

"I think I might handle the situation here better than you."

"What . . . is this place?"

"It can't be what it appears, but I'm damned if I can give you an answer. We'll find out soon enough."

The covey of youngsters grew as it followed them to the center of town. Their shrill voices made bird chirps in the thin mountain air. A few of the promenading gentle ladies turned to watch them pass. By the time they reached the flag-flying building, four men rose from a weathered wooden bench with wrought-iron frame and legs to greet them. One, O'Grady noted with a frown, wore the uniform tunic and trousers of a Confederate cavalry officer, complete with folded-brim gray hat and black plume.

"Howdy. You folks lose your way?" he inquired.

"No," O'Grady answered. "We got forced off the high road to Monterrey by the storm yesterday. This way was open and we thought we might be able to join up with the other further on."

"Sure enough. Y'all can do that. We don't get many visitors to Leesburg, don't encourage them, matter of fact."

"We won't be staying. All we need is time and a place to dry out all our belongings, rest the horses and ourselves, and have a good hot meal."

"You're in my debt, suh. My apologies. Anson Stilwell, at your service, suh. I'm the mayor of this fine community. I will see that your needs are tended to at once."

"Canyon O'Grady," the government agent replied. Before he could go on, Stilwell interrupted.

"The young lady, suh? Is she a native of these parts, or an American like yourself?"

" 'The young lady,' " Mercedes snapped waspishly, "can hear, understand, and speak English."

"Pardon, ma'am," Stilwell said with equanimity. "To whom do I have the pleasure of speaking?"

"Mercedes Elena Fernández y Obregón," she delivered with pounds of ice on each word.

"Of the Coahuila Fernándezes?" Mercedes nodded coldly. "It is indeed an honor. I have had many dealings over cattle with your, ah—father is it?—Don Pedro. You are most welcome here. Tell me, how is your father?"

"My father is dead, along with my elder brothers," Mercedes spat icily. "They were killed by gringo soldiers. I see many men here with parts of uniforms like those who plundered our village wore. Are they perhaps the men we seek?"

That explained it, O'Grady realized. Initially he had been puzzled by Mercedes' reaction. "I'm certain we can say they're not," he assured his companion. "Kilgore and his men wear blue uniforms." To the men before him he made a request. "Can we arrange to stable our horses and get lodging for the night? Our gear should be dry by tomorrow."

"Certainly, suh. My son will show you to the livery and then you can find refreshments at Bolliver's Tavern. Mr. Bolliver lets rooms above his establishment." He made a beckoning gesture and one of the towheaded youngsters stepped forward.

"That will do fine," O'Grady replied, relieved to end the tense conversation.

With the horses cared for, O'Grady led Mercedes to the spacious veranda of the restaurant and tavern. It had been constructed in the style of an antebellum Georgia plantation mansion, complete with flagstoned court between the side wings. There, white-painted tables and chairs, with shade umbrellas in place, provided shelter for guests of the inn. Their host, Mr. Beauregard Bolliver, welcomed them effusively and showed them to a table. A white-jacketed Mexican waiter arrived and Bolliver called for mint juleps around. He noticed his guests' hard looks at the young Mexican and hastened to clarify the situation.

"No, sir, we no longer keep slaves." Mood brightening, he continued, "Sit down, now, sit down, y'all," he burbled. "It is so rare we get visitors from outside the valley. I'm dyin', as I know everyone else is, to hear the news from *outside*." He made the rest of the world sound like a mysterious place.

"In the case of our own country," O'Grady began, accepting the role of news-bringer, "Reconstruction continues in the South. Many persons outside the South, particularly in the West, where I came from, consider the measures taken by federal occupation troops to be entirely too repressive. There is talk of petitioning President Johnson to end it altogether."

"I'm glad to hear that. The Recent Unpleasantness took a terrible enough toll, without adding that barbaric insult to a conquered people. I sometimes think that if only the money cabal's plot to assassinate Lincoln had failed, none of it would have happened."

O'Grady found himself treading on most unsteady ground. "Perhaps. Booth *was* a Southern sympathizer, no one can deny that."

"Certainly not, sir. Unfortunately, creative persons, those of great talent, are often dreadfully unworldly in the realm of politics and intrigue. Those responsible for killing Mr. Lincoln took advantage of Booth's ardent nature and oftstated sympathies to manipulate him to their own ends. Then they abandoned him like the craven demigods they are. Ah! But that is too dreary a subject. The ladies will want to know of the latest fashions. Are you able to satisfy their curiosity, Miss Fernández?"

"Yes, of course. I would be happy to."

"You are most kind. Now, sir, what of the westward

expansion? Are the Indians still wreaking their havoc on the frontier?"

"To some extent, yes. So long as the government honors its treaties, there shouldn't be any more large-scale trouble," O'Grady informed him.

"Humph! If that government would have honored the letter and spirit of the Constitution, there never would have been a War of the Secession."

"Maybe in the South you did not hear of the Red Cloud treaty in sixty-four?" O'Grady inserted to keep the conversation on safer ground.

"No, no, I don't believe we did."

"Red Cloud and the principal chiefs of the Sioux Nation signed a treaty that gave them their sacred Black Hills in Dakota Territory, also the land from there to the Yellowstone, to share with the Cheyenne. They had delivered several humiliating defeats on Union commanders and it seemed wise at the time to treat with the Indians rather than fight another war."

"If anything, Lincoln was a prudent man," Bolliver allowed grudgingly. "Of course he was aware that the Cherokee Nation, the Creek and Seminole, had declared war on the United States and sided with the Confederacy. Better to keep more Indians out of the game than risk defeat. I'm sure he saw it that way."

"No doubt. Now, tell me something. Your flag, the obvious sympathy for a dead cause we see here, has left me wondering. Are all of you former Confederates?"

Bolliver smiled and nodded affirmatively, raising his chilled pewter tumbler to sip of the julep. "All but some twenty Mexican families, and those of ours born here, suh. The entire population of this valley consists of unreconstructed Rebels. Our Mexican friends fled the tyranny of Maximilian. We menfolk, smarting under the evils of Reconstruction, most of us with our property forfeit to the carpetbaggers for falsified taxes, gathered our wives, children, horses, and dogs and headed to Texas. Even on the frontier we found the avaricious, clutching hands of the New England plunderers. So we turned south into Mexico."

"This valley is yours, then? You own the land?"

"Certainly. Many of us served the cause of Benito Juárez to oust the imperialists. Grateful for a cadre of professional soldiers, the new president gave us our land by grant deed. It is ours in perpetuity."

"There's a new danger in this part of Mexico," O'Grady prompted.

Bolliver produced a saddened expression. "So we've heard. A band of brigands under a disgraced Yankee officer. Trash, suh, fit only for the dung heaps of Hades." He drank again. "We should have Anse here if we're going to talk of the present in Mexico. I'll send for him. You met him, of course, outside the town hall, he's the mayor."

Anson Stilwell, filled with energy, a man younger than the careworn features and prematurely gray hair would indicate, bounded in, charged on the prospect of outside news and eager to meet the visitors in a more relaxed atmosphere. When O'Grady and Mercedes rose to greet him, he extended a large work-roughened hand.

"Please, sit down. Beau, send a boy for one of those for me, will you?"

Once seated at the table, Stilwell inquired of their purpose in being in the mountains. O'Grady decided on bluntness.

"We're following after the renegade troops and their leader, Colonel Judson Kilgore. They have been sacking villages in Chihuahua, Coahuila, and here in Nuevo León."

"I've heard of a renegade U.S. Army officer and his large band of marauders. The news disturbs me." In a sudden mood shift, he spoke hotly of his opinion. "They're like Butcher Sherman's 'Bummers,' more inclined to attack women and children, interested solely in loot. Not soldiers, but murderous scavengers."

"I won't take exception to most of what you said. But I would point out," O'Grady continued tactfully, "Kilgore has deserted from the army, he's not representing it or our country down here."

"Hmm. True enough."

Conversation went a dozen ways after this exchange. Dinner plans were made, rooms acquired for Canyon and Mercedes, and a town meeting to hear the news of outside laid out. All without anyone leaving the table. By the time the inn's steward announced the meal, O'Grady felt more than a slight bit tipsy. Their evening of telling the news went well enough. They both retired in exhaustion and slept soundly.

The next morning, O'Grady saw to it they departed early.

They would, he informed Mercedes, have breakfast on the trail. Refreshed, he led out at a brisk pace. Shortly before nine o'clock and the breakfast stop, he announced suddenly, "From the attitude of those volunteer exiles, toward the Union and Yankees in general, I consider them as much a hazard as a chance encounter with unfriendly Mexican authorities. We'll do well to stay clear of them."

Mercedes, glowing from a night of solid slumber, nodded quietly. She didn't understand the politics of any country. Confident that O'Grady did, she was content to leave the matter to him. What she sought lay ahead, not in the past.

12

Clear skies and a warm sun had returned to the mountains. Through another saddle at the eastern end of the Confederates' valley, Canyon O'Grady and Mercedes Fernández regained the main road. They appeared to be the only travelers so far. When the grade increased into the higher reaches of the Sierra Madre, Mercedes expressed a concern that had troubled her for a while.

"Will Miguel be able to join us with the road closed by storm damage?"

O'Grady considered it a moment. He, too, had speculated on the young *hidalgo*'s chances. "He may not. Which is why we spent so much time discussing alternative approaches. Right now I think we should concentrate on finding Kilgore's army, then worry about how to deal with them."

Noon found them looking at ramparts that appeared to have no passage through them. "Don't worry," O'Grady assured his companion. "There has to be a way. Monterrey is on the far side. From here on we had best pick our path with care."

Providence had smiled on Judson Kilgore. The storm and resultant isolation had aided in consolidating their hold on

Villadolor. On the day they had taken the town, the plan he and Lance Means had devised worked to perfection. Only a dozen locals died in the brief fight, including the mayor, the police prefect, and a few imprudent townsmen. Three of the original band had been wounded and two Mexican bandits killed. Since then Kilgore had devoted his energies to strengthening the fortifications of the town.

Villadolor proved to be a larger community than Kilgore had expected. Nine thousand people inhabited the walled city perched on a knob overlooking the high road through the Sierra Madre Oriental. In addition to the cathedral on the plaza, three other churches tended the souls of the residents. There were five cantinas, six inns, and numerous business places. Fine pottery was produced in a large factory that backed against the steep slope of a promontory behind the town. Several blocks boasted the high-walled residences of the wealthy. The rest of the population had employment and lived well, if not prosperously. Even the heavy hand of his occupation force did little to alter daily life. In his new lair, Kilgore planned his future with the help of Captain Means.

"We've stumbled upon a gem here, Lance," Kilgore announced. Seated in the deceased mayor's large leather-upholstered chair, he waved a hand at the maps spread on a large oak table. "All traffic to and from Monterrey flows past this town. From its walls, with swift sallies out by mounted troops, we can control everything that goes on."

Means furrowed his brow. "I've never been comfortable with static defenses. Any fort or city can be put under siege. Mobility is the key to victory."

"Under most conditions, yes." Kilgore rose and walked to the floor-to-ceiling window behind the dead mayor's desk. His glance summoned Means to join him. "Tell me where a besieging army would set up camp."

He gestured toward a narrow strip of meadow across the road from the city walls. At the far edge of its hundred-yard width, a sheer drop-off of five hundred feet separated it from the mountain peak beyond.

"There's not a spot of ground that isn't under fire from the walls," Kilgore concluded grandly.

Captain Means muttered something about roadblocks beyond the bends and flying squads, yet offered no serious rebuttal. His gaze lowered to the plaza outside the building.

There Sergeant Nally and an imperialist recently promoted to NCO rank chatted amiably with several local girls.

"It looks as though romance is in the air," he observed.

"Eh?"

"Our men have taken to fraternizing with the locals. Nally will have that leggy one in his bunk before sundown, I'll wager."

Kilgore grunted uncomfortably. "So long as they keep in mind that we are the conquerors and the women the conquered. Spoils of war, eh? I suppose we can't deny them their, ah, recreations. Now, to our defenses," he changed subject briskly. "I want the work on the primary and secondary walls completed by the end of the week. There will need to be a company armory on each of the three sides. Which reminds me, is the house-to-house search for weapons going according to plan?"

"Yes, sir," Means answered a bit stiffly.

"Results?" Kilgore asked craftily.

"A dozen rifles located so far, two old fusils, a brace of horse pistols. Those people are not accustomed to freely owning firearms, Jud. Most of what we've found are shotguns, what they call *escopetas*."

"I'm about to create a maxim," Kilgore stated, then chuckled at the pompous sound of it. "A shotgun can get a man a Spencer carbine, and a carbine can get him seven more. Given to six of his friends, the seven carbines can get forty-nine more. Hell, to take it one step further, a knife can get a shotgun, which can get a carbine, which can get, and so forth. That's why I want all weapons in the hands of the locals confiscated. That way they have no choice but to obey us."

Impressed, Means whistled softly. "I'd not considered it that way. Speaking of carbines, we may have a solution to the ammunition shortage. That imperialist—ah—Captain de Vega has a couple of metalworkers among his entourage. He and they have been talking to the coppersmith here in town and it appears we can set up an ammunition factory. They've already started on gang molds for the bullets, there's plenty of powder available in kegs, and the mine behind town is a source for fulminate from blasting caps."

"Brilliant. Excellent use of resources, Lance. I commend

you for it and I'll mention it to de Vega later today. What's
next?"

"The officers' mess has a problem . . ." Means began.

At first glance, the walled city that rose into view beyond
a steep grade in the road had all the charm of a fabled city
of Europe in the Middle Ages. Spires and towers rose
above the crenellated walls, which appeared to be perched
on a flat-topped, rounded bastion of the mountain which
formed a backdrop. Mercedes brightened and started to
urge her horse to a faster gait.

"I've heard about this place. Villadolor, though I don't
know why the gloomy name. Hurry, let's get there early.
There are supposed to be marvelous posadas and restau-
rants in Villadolor, shops of all sorts, a center for artists
and potters."

O'Grady's hand on the reins halted her exuberance.
"Hold on. Take a careful look at that place. What do you
see?"

Mercedes studied it, her amber eyes sparkling in anticipation, arched ebon brows drawn together. "It looks peaceful
and prosperous. Men are working on the wall. It . . . it's
like a fairy-tale castle."

"Maybe I should have asked what you didn't see,"
O'Grady amended. "One out of all those spires has to be
the center of government. That one, I'd say, across from
the cathedral. Do you see the Mexican flag flying?"

"Uh-no. What does that mean?"

"If the flag isn't flying at the Edificio Municipal, then I
think we can be fairly sure we've found Kilgore and his
bandits."

"But . . . a town this size? They couldn't possibly capture
it."

"Not by assault, possibly. Kilgore's clever. He could have
used subterfuge. Whatever the case, Mercedes my lass, I
think we should leave the road here and scout the place a
bit more before riding in."

Over the next two hours O'Grady and Mercedes worked
their way through the thick forest, observing Villadolor
from a safe distance. They remained unobserved as they
took stock of men strengthening the battlements of the
outer glacis facing the road, while others repaired the ban-

quettes. Other workers punched holes in the blank face of the building walls that formed the inner parapet.

O'Grady counted fully fifty armed men supervising the work of some two hundred laborers. From beyond the walls, the sound of hammers and saws kept a steady rhythm. The three cannon—he surmised them to be six-pounders— held no threat for him. No one would fire a powder eater like that at a single target. Sentries stood at the three large gates that allowed access to the interior. In all, he found it more of a challenge than desirable. Perhaps he was fortunate that a larger body of vengeance-hungry Mexican men hadn't come with him. After looking down into the town from the mountain slope behind Villadolor, O'Grady made a decision.

"Let's draw back, beyond that bend and into the forest a bit. We'll make camp and then I want a closer look at what's inside there."

"How can you?" Mercedes blurted, then realized what he had in mind. "It's too dangerous, Canyon."

O'Grady produced a bleak smile. "Danger is what I'm paid to encounter, lass. Come on, now. We have to cover our tracks."

Camped at a safe distance from the fortress, O'Grady and Mercedes waited while the sun slowly slid toward the western sky. She heated water for coffee, put on a pan of reconstituted *machaca*, with chiles, onions, and beans.

"How can I convince you not to go?" she asked while stirring the mixture.

"You can't," O'Grady answered simply.

"What makes you think you can get in there unnoticed?"

"I'll be showin' you that in a minute," he responded, rising and walking to the gear from the packsaddle.

From the pile he selected the long flat ironbound case and carried it to where Mercedes knelt. He opened it and began to draw out items he considered would help his intended penetration.

"In here are some items I brought along that I thought might prove helpful. There's a pair of trousers, Union Army blue, with cavalry stripe, a kepi, a wool shirt, a regulation pistol belt and holster. Wearing these, I should be able to walk right in the front gate."

Mercedes opened her mouth to protest, but said nothing. She, too, was learning.

* * *

"Halt! Who goes there?" the slovenly young sentry at the main gate to Villadolor demanded, snapping out of his slouched sitting position to menace the figure walking toward the gate.

"It's Donahue, you blind bastard," O'Grady growled at him. He swaggered in out of the lowering twilight, right hand resting easily on the closed flap holster at his waist.

"Sorry, Sergeant, I didn't recognize you without your chevrons."

Well, he'd been promoted. "That's all you stupid whelp privates ever look at, isn't it? Me stripes. Put stripes on a donkey and ye'd be doin' his bidding," O'Grady grumped as he stalked through the gate, head averted to prevent the inexperienced sentry from getting a good look.

"Sometimes I think we already are," an anonymous voice called from the shadow of the wall.

"Damn yer black heart, I'll have yer guts for garters," O'Grady bellowed in good imitation of an Irish sergeant.

Through a tunnellike passage formed by a three-story house, he found himself inside the town. So far, no problem. Now to set about learning what he had come for.

A midafternoon sun burned down when a party of five young officers in the outlaw army abruptly rode out of the trees and into the campsite O'Grady had left an hour before. They startled Mercedes, who was cleaning the cooking utensils. Mutual shock afflicted the youthful soldiers, who had been seeking game to supplement their monotonous rations at the officers' mess.

"Lord God, look what we've got here," newly promoted Captain Edward Kilgore gulped.

His pale complexion, accentuated by long glossy black hair, pomaded and parted in the middle, flushed with the sudden birth of ardor. He regarded the attractive young woman, frozen in a crouch, with a naked hunger. His watery eyes, an indistinct blue-gray, glittered with cunning and lust.

"Who is she?" one companion asked, gaping at the beautiful Mercedes.

"I don't know, and it doesn't really matter," Edward told him. "She's Mexican and she's in our area of operations, so that makes her fair game." He started to dismount, an erection already pressing the front of his trousers.

"Hey, let's don't just hump her and leave her," another lieutenant suggested. "Why not . . . why not take her back to the mess?"

His idea caught with two more. "Sure. We could use more than one kind of fresh meat in that place."

"We have a whole town from which to pick and choose," Edward protested. He wanted to wet his wick right now. "Why bother taking this one back?"

"I'll tell you why. Because I don't want sloppy seconds, or thirds, or whatever you leave for me, Eddie," a belligerent voice countered.

By then Mercedes had recovered herself. She rose, a ten-inch cast-iron skillet in one hand. *"Soldados?"* she asked wonderingly, as though the idea had never occurred to her. For some reason she felt it wise not to reveal to these evil-looking youths that she understood English. "Get out of here," she went on, brandishing the skillet. "Go away, leave me alone."

Two others dismounted and began circling wide, to close in from both directions. Eddie Kilgore advanced on her. His grin did nothing to make his sallow face more pleasant. Behind him a lieutenant with a dead deer slung over his saddle chuckled softly.

Separated from her rifle and revolver, Mercedes raised her sole weapon menacingly. "Stay away. If you hurt me, my husband will punish you severely."

"What's she sayin'?" one tormentor demanded.

"Hell'f I know," Eddie responded. "That gabble-gabble Mexican turkey talk don't mean nothing to me. All I know is I want to hoist up that riding skirt and give her eight inches of pleasure."

"Eight!" his original detractor blared rudely. "You and what other two fellers, Eddie?"

"Shut up, Steve. A lot you know." Eddie Kilgore pouted.

"I've been talkin' with Rosita at the mess," Steve taunted.

"That's enough, I told you," Eddie snarled.

"She says she's seen ten-year-olds—"

"God damn you, Steve!" Eddie bellowed as he turned swiftly, revolver half clear of the flap holster.

"Rein it in, both of you," an older officer snapped. "No

room for the bullshit. Just relax. I vote with the majority, we'll take her in and share her around in the mess.''

"But I want to pump her now, right now, here in the woods. Geez, I'm so stiff my pecker aches.''

"Let it ache a little longer, Eddie. Gates are likely to be locked against us when we do arrive.''

"All right,'' Eddie relented nastily. "You two grab her and let's put her on a horse.''

Mercedes swung the cast-iron skillet. It made a bonging sound when it struck one of her abductors on the elbow. He howled with pain and staggered back a step. The second outlaw officer caught her by the wrist and wrenched the deadly metal object from her grasp. Eddie Kilgore advanced on her.

"Behave, you little bitch, or we'll take turns on you right here until you bleed, then leave you to die,'' he snarled. Hard, powerful blows to both cheeks emphasized his threat.

Mercedes bit the inside of her lower lip to prevent any outcry. Furious, yet cautious enough not to reveal her reason for being there, Mercedes continued to resist their attempts to remove her. Eddie Kilgore moved in and backhanded her twice. The cracking blows reddened her cheeks. Balling his fist, Eddie punched Mercedes hard in the solar plexus.

Breath rushed from her and blackness rolled down behind her eyes. With a soft grunt, Mercedes sagged into the waiting arms of Eddie Kilgore. He enlisted the aid of the closest two to dump her over his saddle bow. He gave her temptingly rounded posterior a couple of pats and jigged the reins.

"Back to town,'' he commanded.

13

O'Grady entered the Plaza de Armas filled with confidence. He had left the central square for last. So far he had located three buildings obviously used for armories. That would make blowing them up for a diversion more difficult and would not wipe out all the enemy's ammunition in a single effort. From inside, the new construction work had been obvious.

It appeared Judson Kilgore intended on a long stay. Perhaps he considered this the ideal private kingdom. He couldn't do much better, O'Grady admitted. From Mercedes he had learned that the road that passed by Villadolor, for want of rail connections, carried all the traffic between the silver mines around Durango in the Sierra Madre Occidental and Monterrey. Also nearly all other commerce that had to traverse the Sierra Madre Oriental. So long as the Mexican Army could be held off, Kilgore could enjoy a long and profitable sojourn in Villadolor.

"Which is what I have to prevent," O'Grady reminded himself in a whisper.

He turned toward the Edificio Municipal, reviewing what he had learned so far. Most disconcerting was the realization that Kilgore's effective force now exceeded one hundred and fifty. A raw wooden barracks under construction gave evidence of this. As he approached the city offices, a new factor disturbed him greatly. Although no Mexican banner flew from the jackstaff atop the spire, there was a flag.

Jutting at a thirty-degree angle from the plastered pillar outside the street-width main gate into the courtyard of the Edificio Municipal hung a large scarlet ensign, on which had been embroidered a representation of a death's-head and a clenched mailed fist. Apparently Kilgore knew of the sobriquet, Coronel Muerte, and gloried in it. The hateful emblem gave O'Grady a chill. If Kilgore kept this up, he might start winning over large numbers of followers. The President had warned him that Kilgore possessed imagination and initiative.

He would, he now accepted, have to exercise his own to the utmost degree. For all his determination to handle this assignment alone and secretively, he now accepted the need of Miguel Fernández and his ex-soldier volunteers. The defenses, sheer number of opponents, and the apparent willingness of the townspeople to allow Kilgore's horde within their walls demanded it. He could, of course, fall back on the final solution.

President Johnson had made it abundantly clear that he was to bring Kilgore out of Mexico dead if he could not manage to do so alive. Assassination had a dirty taste in Canyon O'Grady's mouth. It reminded him too clearly of a man he admired greatly. Abraham Lincoln had deserved far better than a cowardly assassin's bullet. O'Grady and his unknown number of brother agents had striven for years to prevent any harm to the President, as had Alan Pinkerton and his small force. In the end, one of Lincoln's most admired theatrical personalities had fired the fatal shot. Sure, there would have to be another way, O'Grady promised himself. He was no John Wilkes Booth.

Raucous shouts from a large cantina on one side of the square reminded him that there had been a dramatic increase in the officer corps. Overheard conversations and envious remarks had apprised him of the fact that Captain Lancelot Means had been promoted to major, along with a man named El Carnicero—the Butcher—and another Mexican, a former imperialist by the name of Hernán de Vega. Four men, two of the original American deserters, two Mexican, had been made captains, and there were fresh lieutenants among the officer corps.

"Eddie's bringing us a surprise," a whiskey-raw voice yelled inside the cantina that served as the officers' mess.

"Oh, what's that?"

"I'm not sure, though he did say it had tits."

"You gotta hand it to him." The drunk waxed sentimental. "Eddie's good people, even if he's the Old Man's kid."

"Another of these Mex-Indian doxies, I'll wager," a disgruntled officer complained.

"Here he comes, he's comin' now," another of Kilgore's "gentlemen" shouted.

Following a jostle in the crowd, a roar of approval greeted Eddie Kilgore's arrival. O'Grady cast a frowning visage that direction, unaware that Mercedes was the cause for their festivity. His reconnaissance incomplete, he decided to give the church a try.

Votive candles flickered in a bank twenty rose-tinted glass containers long and five ranks high. Few other than the old women came to the church since the bandit mob had struck the town. Among the children, none of the boys over ten came at all. Father Antonio Pérez, his elbows resting on the dark wooden ledge of a *prie-dieu* to the right of the high altar, could have wept with frustration and defeat.

These murderers, thieves, plunderers, men without conscience or conviction, had seduced away his flock more effectively than all the other snares of Satan. He had to make do with little lads not old enough or practiced enough to be other than clumsy as altar boys. He heard no confessions except the childish lisps of these youngsters, the girls, and the old women. He baptized no babies, though four had been born since the outlaws came. Temptation to cry out in righteous wrath against the defilers forced a sigh that approximated a sob.

When it came down to it, he hadn't a single strong right arm to defend him if he were to make public complaint or deliver a homily that denounced the invaders. And, guiltily, Father Antonio had to admit he didn't consider himself ready for martyrdom. That's why he gasped with sudden fear and shock when a tall broad-shouldered man entered the nave. When the military kepi, which marked him as one of the evil throng, came off, the priest dimly saw a shock of bright red hair in the wavering yellow of candlelight.

To Padre Antonio's wonder, the man dipped into the holy-water font and crossed himself, walked slowly up the aisle, and genuflected before the crucified Christ on his cross and then turned to the cleric.

"Been doing a big business since our Yanqui friends have come to town, padre?" the visitor asked in fairly polished Spanish.

Another surprise. "N-no, my son. Hardly, as you should know. H-how is it that one of so hard and diabolical a company would find time to visit the church?" his bitterness made him ask in English.

"Don't let appearances deceive you, Father," O'Grady urged in the same language. "I am not of this town, nor one of those."

Confusion and unease rattled the priest. "Then what . . . ? How . . . ? Why . . . are you here?"

"Truth to tell, Father, I wanted another perspective on what is going on. How solidly do these bandit scum control the town? Would anyone raise a hand to resist them?"

"You talk like a soldier," Father Antonio accused.

"I assure you I am not. Though I do seek to find the enemy's weaknesses. Say it's for my own reasons."

"Surely you can trust me with such—"

O'Grady lifted a hand to terminate the flow of words. "I wouldn't want to burden you with information that could be personally dangerous. For now be satisfied that not all of Mexico is in fear of your Colonel Muerte, nor enthralled by him. Help is on the way. Now, padre, if you would answer my questions, I'll be out of here and leave you to your devotions."

Quickly O'Grady ran down his list of wants. His heart fluttering with renewed hope, Father Antonio provided the answers. O'Grady thanked him and slipped unobtrusively out the side door of the baptistery. Now all he had to do was get safely out of there.

At a side-street cantina, O'Grady acquired four buckets of beer and a newspaper-wrapped package of warm tamales. These accompanied him through the plaza and down the main street to the high gate fronting the road. The sentry, observing his burdens, inquired what he had in mind, leaving so near dark.

"Carin' for me lads, boy. That picket post is dry and hungry work." So saying, he walked unmolested out the main portal and into the dark night.

Spying was hungry work. Back at the place he had left his palomino, O'Grady ate three of the thick meat-filled cornmeal rolls and drank one bucket of beer. The remains he hid in the brush, mounted, and walked Cormac out into the forest. He kept to a game trail by which he had evaded the picket post established on the road. Nightfall slipped over him with mountain suddenness. When he reached the campsite, he found Mercedes missing.

Baffled by this, O'Grady searched the area. She was not at the creek, bathing, as he expected. He found her horse on his second cast through camp. He knew better than to call her name. Lighting a shuttered Banner oil lamp, he began to search the ground. Where in hell had she gone?

Near the tree line on the north side of the clearing, O'Grady found five distinct sets of hoofprints. One animal seemed to be carrying more weight than the others. He followed them around to the left, then near to the fire ring. He made out footprints then, different from his own or those of the beautiful Mercedes.

Someone had come and taken her off. Not without a struggle, O'Grady deduced. Satisfied, he followed the departing tracks to the edge of the clearing at the east. It left little doubt as to the direction taken.

"Aw, dammit now," he breathed aloud, certain of her destination if not her fate.

A rustle of brush drew his attention behind him. He turned the beam of the Banner lamp as he pivoted.

Two men eased out of the trees, weapons held casually in his direction. One kept him covered while his companion dismounted, then took his turn. They wore enough faded bits of uniform to identify themselves to O'Grady.

"Looks like Eddie was right," one informed the other. "We done found her man. Hey, Mex," he continued in atrocious Spanish, "what're you doin' in U.S. Army duds?"

"I . . . I found them, *señores*," O'Grady stammered, playing the role they expected of him, gambling for time. "Where . . . where is my woman?"

"Well, now, that's nothing to concern you anymore," the other deserter said in English. "Tell him that, Tad."

O'Grady saw the officers' insigne on both their tunics. He stiffened when the one without Spanish spoke again. "Well, Eddie sent us back here to dispose of this chile slurper, we might as well get on with it."

He needed time! "Why is the whereabouts of my woman of no importance, *señores*?"

"He-he," Tad chuckled. "Well, greaser," he began in English, then switched to his outlandish Spanish. "We took that hot little Mex number off to our officers' bar to work as a whore. And since we're gonna kill you, you don't have to worry about what happens to her."

O'Grady tried to stifle his hot, angry reaction, but the outlaw soldiers saw it and interpreted it correctly. In a fleeting instant they swung their weapons into line.

They're going to kill you, O'Grady, his mind yammered at him. Spurred by that knowledge, Canyon O'Grady acted quickly. His gun hand sure and swift, he had the Colt Model '60 clear of leather before either opponent realized it, in spite of the flap holster.

"Wrong, boys," he snarled in clear English.

Triggering his revolver, he watched in the accelerated time sense of combat as the hammer fell on a percussion cap in slow motion. Flame spurted from the muzzle, blue-white smoke right behind. A black spot, red-splashed, appeared in the center of Tad's chest. Tad rocked backward as the .44-caliber ball splintered his sternum and sent slivers of bone into his lungs.

"Jesus, I'm hit," Tad wailed weakly.

Already O'Grady had gone into motion. He dodged right, dropped, and rolled. He came up blasting a second round into the open mouth of the wounded man. A jink to the left and he flopped behind a rock. A slug screamed off into the night, flattened and deflected by the granite boulder.

"It won't be you doing the killing," O'Grady taunted.

It had the desired effect. The second young officer showed himself to get a better shot. O'Grady put a ball between his ribs on the right side. He did a pratfall and stared stupidly at O'Grady, who came from behind the boulder. Only when his reeling brain recorded the black hole of the Colt's muzzle pointed at his head did he show any sign of human emotion. Tears welled up and spilled down his face.

Gritting his teeth, O'Grady shot him anyway.

He worked fast then. From Tad, who was near his size, he removed the officer's insigne, trousers, and gauntlets. Then he dragged the corpses into the woods and removed any trace of them in the camp. Grimly he donned his new persona and dusted off his clothing. This disguise had worked once, he considered; it should serve a second time.

14

Wearing the epaulets of an officer, Canyon O'Grady had no difficulty getting through the gate, already closed for the night. Again he left Cormac outside Villadolor, this time along a side wall, for he had little hope of departing the way he had entered. On the plaza, loud music still blared from the cantina designated as the officers' mess. O'Grady headed directly there.

Local musicians strolled between the tables in the inner courtyard; guitars, a violin, a cornet, and a small portable harp. Piano music tinkled from the main barroom. Young women, all locals, crowded around the officers of Kilgore's army and the prosperous businessmen of Villadolor who had eagerly collaborated with the enemy. O'Grady figured that their outlook had to be that no matter who ran things, so long as they made a profit and lived well, it beat hell out of being dead. He stepped up to the bar.

"Give me a beer," he ordered, the English sounding strange in his ears.

So far his entrance to the crowded saloon had hardly been noted. One young officer at the bar, who was standing his friends drinks, proved the exception. He glanced at O'Grady in a casual way and turned away. Then he returned his gaze in a penetrating and speculative manner. He said a few words to his companions, unheard over the general noise, and pushed away from the rail. He walked up to O'Grady and stopped, legs wide apart, one hand on a hip.

"I don't believe I've seen you in here before," Edward Kilgore challenged. "But I have seen you."

O'Grady took in his interrogator's long black locks and slightly effeminate features. "That's possible, Captain," he answered blandly.

Edward squinted, pursed his lips. "Yes, yes, of course. I've seen you as an enlisted man."

A tense silence spread outward from the point where they stood. O'Grady calculated his dwindling odds. Then he noted how bright and shiny-new the captain's twin silver bars appeared. Also the fact the young man had been buying drinks. Obviously he had been one of the recent promotions.

"As a sergeant," O'Grady corrected. "I was promoted just today."

Immediately the tension eased in Edward Kilgore. His face made a transition to a beaming smile and he clapped O'Grady on one shoulder. "Why, so have I. Congratulations. This calls for a celebration. Come, have a drink with us."

Tinkling notes came from the piano again and the clatter of voices filled the room. Edward Kilgore led the way to where his cronies stood at the far end of the mahogany. He called loudly for a round, then turned to announce the plans he had formulated in the past minute.

"We're going to have a feast, gentlemen. The best the house has to offer, with lots of wine and song and lovely ladies. You're all invited to help me and my friend here, ah—"

"O'Grady," Canyon supplied.

"—*Lieutenant* O'Grady and me celebrate our elevation in rank. And let me tell you now, O'Grady, you're in for a real treat after we've exhausted all the other diversions."

"Eddie, what you got in mind?" one of the subalterns inquired.

Edward waggled an admonitory finger under the questioner's nose. "I wouldn't be anything if I weren't my father's son. And a Kilgore is always generous to a fault, right? So . . . I'm going to give *Lieutenant* O'Grady here the privilege of . . . the extreme privilege of . . . No. I'll save that for later. It'll be my secret until after we dine. Now, if one of you who speak this barbarian language will call the cantinero, we'll order our repast."

Trapped by Kilgore's alcoholic camaraderie, O'Grady had no choice other than to play along. Somewhere in the building, he knew, Mercedes had to be confined, or worse, pressed into service as a prostitute. When he had first learned this, he could have choked on his rage; now he had grown cold, calculated in his thoughts. While maintaining a jovial exterior, he simmered in his most dangerous state.

Several small square tables were shoved together in the patio to accommodate the party. Waiters bustled around. The food, when it came, was excellent. With aching suddenness O'Grady recalled that he had eaten nothing except the tamales since early afternoon. He relaxed his guard enough to savor the viands as huge clay bowls of *biftec ranchero* and *carnitas* came to the table.

He ate sparingly, conscious of impending demands for swift action, while the others gorged. After all had consumed their fill, and brandy-laced coffee went the rounds, Edward Kilgore rose and called for attention.

"And now for our special treat for a brand-new lieutenant. Only today we acquired a delightful and spirited addition to the covey of beauties abovestairs. It is my intention to present as a gift to our fine new lieutenant the first enjoyable fruits of that fair slip of a girl." He turned to one of the revelers. "Johnny, go fetch her down."

O'Grady fought his inclinations during the delay while the mildly inebriated young lieutenant climbed the stairs to a typical balcony that surrounded the patio. O'Grady noted that with the exception of two, all the doors had been removed and replaced with hanging draperies. Above this level the third floor appeared to be sleeping quarters for the officers. Quickly he tried to formulate a plan.

Damn, he didn't know enough about the building, O'Grady realized as Johnny reappeared from one of the locked rooms, dragging Mercedes by one wrist. Even from this distance, O'Grady saw that she glared at her escort with caustic malevolence. With halting progress the pair made their way to the patio. Johnny brought the young woman to where Edward stood, amid soft whistles of appreciation.

"Well, wench, it's time for you to commence your duties." Edward Kilgore sneered. "To do that, I'm making you a gift to a dear friend and newly commissioned officer . . ."

Her defiance wasted, Mercedes stood at the table with her head down. Edward's next words brought her chin up in a swift movement that shook her long black hair in rolling waves. ". . . Lieutenant O'Grady."

Barely able to conceal her shock and surprise, Mercedes fought to mold her face into an expression of disgust and disdain. It seemed a dream to her. How had O'Grady gotten here? Had he really changed sides? Grinning, O'Grady rose and walked to the head of the table. He accepted Mercedes' hand from Edward Kilgore and led her toward the nearest flight of stairs that led to the curtained mezzanine.

Diagonally across the plaza from the officers' quarters and mess, a light glowed in the second-floor window of what had been the mayor's office. The dark, richly glowing paneling that stretched from floor to ceiling gave the room a somber atmosphere. Heavy wood-and-leather furniture graced the large Oriental rug that covered hand-hewn, lovingly smoothed floorboards. Behind the vast space of a rectangular mahogany desk sat Colonel Judson Kilgore. He met with his new staff officers; the subject at hand concerned progress on the ammunition factory.

"So far we haven't been required to expend any more ammunition," Major Lancelot Means pointed out. "At the rate we're going, we should have the first new lot out by the end of next week."

"I suspect that the reason we've not been called upon to fire up what we have left is that the road west has been blocked until yesterday," Kilgore answered dryly. "If the Mexican government gathers enough courage to send the army after us, it won't be from Monterrey. They'll come from the countryside that has been ravaged. Besides, witnessing the damage will help fire the resolve of the rank and file. Common soldiers need motivation in any army."

"Well put," Means seconded. "Even if they get here before the ammunition is perfected and in good supply, we still have the artillery."

"Every day you experiment with cartridges, the powder supply for those cannon decreases by a small increment," Major de Vega pointed out. "I may be at odds with the current government, but I know my countrymen. Haven't they just proved it? Any call to defend the sacred soil of Mexico is motivation enough. If—no, when—they come, we'll have a great deal of trouble on our hands."

"Nothing we can't handle, let me assure you," Kilgore offered.

"In that I must agree," Major Francisco Bernal—El Carnicero—rumbled from his seat around the desk. "Unlike you"—he made slighting reference to de Vega—"my men and I served the cause of Benito Juárez. I know the internal weakness of these *soldados*."

" 'The cause of Benito Juárez,' " de Vega mocked. "You served the cause of El Carnicero. The troops of Juárez confiscated matériel necessary to the conduct of war. You robbed the helpless villages and the peons in the field of everything they had, in the name of freeing Mexico. A bandido is a bandido is a bandido," he spat.

"Gentlemen, put aside personal difference," Kilgore urged. "We are united· now. We must blend our talents into making the most of our situation. Some people might describe me as a bandit. But I am an empire builder. One without contaminated, corrupted strings to some decrepit European throne. It's my desire to build a truly American empire, and you gentlemen will be my barons and earls."

Hostility still crackled between de Vega and Bernal, allayed only by the arrival of a messenger. He knocked and entered, breathless from a long and hasty ride. "Coronel, I have come from the patrol sent beyond the flood damage. Important news has come to us."

"What is that?" Kilgore asked.

"It is the Durango train. Many wagons, heavy with silver. They are guarded by a company of *lanzeros*. Forty-five soldiers in all. They make necessary road repairs as they progress. They are but three days' ride away from Villadolor."

Eyes widening at this intelligence, Kilgore considered it a long, silent moment. Then he rose from his chair. Knuckles whitening on the surface of the desk, he leaned toward his staff officers.

"Gentlemen, we shall seize this bullion and make it our own. Alert the officers. Cancel all festivities."

Canyon and Mercedes entered one of the drape-shielded cubicles off the mezzanine. She started to speak and he silenced her with a finger to her lips.

"Listen to me. I came to get you out of here."

"How did you know?"

"That stringy-haired animal down there sent two of his friends back to take care of whatever male companion you had in camp. They made the mistake of bragging about it before they carried out their assignment. As it worked out, I killed them first. Now, here's what I want you to do. Start some small talk, anything at first, then make it more—ah—

racy. I'll answer sometimes. While you do, I'll look into getting us away from this place."

"What sort of man are you?" Mercedes said aloud and suddenly. "Let me—let me do this my own way."

"Honey, you've got a nice body there, I just want to see it," O'Grady responded, catching up the theme. Silently he worked his way around the room.

"I . . . I've never done this before."

"Sure you haven't." O'Grady sneered. "Get outta that dress." He located a connecting door to the next room. His nod encouraged her to say more.

Getting into the act, Mercedes loudly rustled her skirt. "Here, here, do you like these?"

"Beautiful. How do you say it? *Las nalgas bonitas*," O'Grady said loudly with a wink.

"Hoo-haw!" came a bray from the patio. "Beautiful tits. Eddie, your pal O'Grady's sure got class."

"It's working," the subject of amusement assured Mercedes as he cautiously turned the knob on the connecting door.

"Ummmm. What's that lump in your pants?" Mercedes cooed loudly.

O'Grady winced. "Don't overdo it." The partition parted and he entered the next chamber.

"Oh!" Mercedes squeaked. "It's . . . it's soooo big."

In the other room, O'Grady discovered a larger opening than their cubicle contained, with a small balcony beyond French doors. He tried the latch handle and it gave freely. He left one panel open and hastily returned to Mercedes.

"We've got a way. We'll have to hurry," he whispered; then, loudly, "You like it, baby? C'mere, let me rub it against you."

"Oh! Oh, please!" Mercedes wailed.

"Let's get in that bed, honey. I'm gonna give you a whole lot of fun."

Together they sat on the contraption of wood, rope, and leather. Bouncing up and down, they produced a satisfactory creaking.

"Oh, please, don't hurt me. Ayeeee, not so fast." Mercedes did an imitation of a reluctant virgin.

Taking her hand, O'Grady led Mercedes to the other room. On the balcony they began to tear strips from the sun-deteriorated drapery. These O'Grady began to knot together. After a moment he nodded toward the vacated cubicle.

"You'll have to carry on alone. Go give them some moans and groans."

"Canyon, you're a beast. But I'll do it because I love you."

Love? That was the first time she had said that, O'Grady thought, his emotions suddenly set awhirl. Better to get back to it. They had too damn little time.

Short and stout, the bowlegged Mexican orderly who entered the officers' mess came smartly to attention and snapped the bugle he carried to his lips. The short staccato call silenced all sounds of pleasure-seeking. Immediately the last note started to fade, Major Means entered the saloon.

"Gentlemen, we're on the eve of a new campaign. One that will prove quite lucrative individually, as well as provide for the needs of the entire company. Officers' call at four o'clock tomorrow morning. You will be expected to be prompt and sober. We will depart the fortress at eight o'clock. All festivities are hereby canceled by order of Colonel Kilgore. This applies particularly to noncommissioned and enlisted ranks. The colonel is sure you gentlemen will set the example. Tattoo in thirty minutes."

"Jesus, what's this?" Johnny asked the table at large.

"You ask me," Eddie Kilgore opined, "it's our first skirmish with the Mexican Army."

"Lord, are we ready?" Lieutenant Frazier asked weakly.

"As much as we'll ever be," Eddie told him.

"Know what I think?" Lieutenant César Domínguez asked. "This is about the time of the spring silver shipment from Durango. I say we're after the bullion."

"Whatever the reason, we'll need our sleep and a tight hand on our troops," Captain Kilgore declared. "I'll cover for our friend O'Grady until he finishes with that delicious piece up there. I think the rest of us should follow the major's suggestion."

"Lucky dog, O'Grady. He gets an extra half-hour to bang away," someone offered enviously.

"I hope he's enjoying it."

"Oh, I'm sure he is, Johnny. No doubt about that," Eddie Kilgore said with a lascivious wink.

15

"That should do it," O'Grady said as he tied off the make-shift rope and tested the hold of the knots.

"You go first," Mercedes suggested.

"No, it'll be better if you do. Any danger will come from inside. Over you go now."

Mercedes swung a leg over the wrought-iron railing and grasped the velvety cloth. With a boost from O'Grady, she had both limbs to twine around the drape and slowly slide to the ground. O'Grady waited until her feet touched the cobbles of the alley, then stepped over onto the ledge and clutched their lifeline. Ankles locked around the material, he made a swift descent.

"That way," he directed, indicating the section of wall beyond which he had tethered Cormac and a spare horse for Mercedes.

"The gate is over there," Mercedes corrected.

"I know it. You heard that announcement. Everything will be shut down now. We wouldn't have a chance."

"What's over there?" she asked, starting in the indicated direction.

"Horses. I had no idea how long it would take to find you and get away from this place."

"Um. You think of everything, Canyon."

"Don't praise me too highly until we get out of here," O'Grady riposted forthrightly.

Five minutes' brisk walk brought them to a place where the buildings ceased and the curtain wall continued like any other battlement. Stone steps gave access to the banquette. Halfway to the top, Mercedes tugged at O'Grady's sleeve.

"How do we get down from here?" she asked.

"Damn." He thought a minute, visualizing objects along their route. "Let's go back to that row of shops. I have an idea."

Along a block that angled toward the wall, ground-floor space had been allotted to businesses of varying sorts. Each had a roll-shutter of stout wood or metal strips that closed off access to the storefronts. When the fugitives reached there, O'Grady drew his belt knife and began to cut away the strong cords that raised and lowered the barriers. Doubling these, he began to tie them together.

"If there are enough of these, our problem is solved," he observed to Mercedes.

"And if we don't?"

"We'll have a drop-off to the ground. Start tying these double strands together while I go get more."

That O'Grady had to have the stamina and self-control of a demon. Half an hour had passed since the pair had gone upstairs, twenty minutes since the institution of curfew. Eddie Kilgore paced the flagstones of the vacated patio. The guy's pecker had to be numb to go this long. He pulled a long thin cheroot from his tunic pocket and bit off the end.

With a hiss and a sulfurous scent like Satan's breath, the lucifer match came to life in Eddie's hand. He let the blob of phosphor and sulfur burn clear before bringing the flame close under the rich, well-cured tobacco. The cigar puffed to a glowing tip. Dammit, enough was enough. O'Grady could have humped his way around the world in this time. Uttering an impatient curse, Eddie Kilgore started for the stairway.

He found the room empty. Had O'Grady somehow managed to sneak past them and take her to his quarters? He saw the open access to the next room. Eddie covered the narrow space in three paces. On the threshold he saw the other room had no occupants. To his right he spotted the open French door. What the hell?

Gripped by a growing suspicion that something terrible lay behind this disappearance, he blundered onto the balcony and immediately saw the dangling drapery cloth. Through the liquor fogging his brain he realized that Tad and Victor had never returned from checking the campsite for the Mexican hussy's companion. Had he bested two armed and competent officers? And was he the redheaded O'Grady?

"God—damn—them!" His anguished bellow echoed off the buildings of the square.

He had been made to look the fool. If not to his brother officers as yet, to himself. Worse, what would he be in the eyes of his father? How could he explain this? What would he say? Gulping back his fear of the senior Kilgore's wrath, Eddie took himself off the balcony and down through the officers' quarters to the plaza. He would have to go to headquarters and report this to his father.

Eddie Kilgore's anguished cry was heard distinctly at the wall where Canyon O'Grady finished the last of the makeshift rope. He cocked his head to one side, listening for more disturbance. When none came, he produced a fleeting smile.

"It appears our Captain Kilgore has discovered he's given me more than he thought he did." To Mercedes, "We have to hurry more than I expected. I've tied it off to that ring bolt. It's bound to be strong enough. You go first—the danger's still behind us."

This time Mercedes did not protest. With only slight hesitation from uncertainty, she straddled the rope, gripped it tightly, and stepped backward off the wall. O'Grady's admonishment came to her barely in time.

"Plant your feet. You want to walk down the wall."

It seemed forever to O'Grady while he divided his attention between the descending woman and the streets behind them. So far nothing stirred. Apparently young Kilgore had not turned out the guard. No, he'd probably want to confer with Daddy first, O'Grady reasoned. He heard a gentle slapping, the signal that the rope was free. Quickly he positioned himself, leaned back to be supported by his arms, and walked toward the ground.

"There, that wasn't too bad," he quipped when he joined Mercedes.

"The other, that sun-rotted drape material, made me worry a lot more," she admitted. "Where are the horses?"

"Over this way," O'Grady directed.

They hastened to where the palomino and her mare waited, heads down, cropping off tufts of grass. Cormac raised his head, whuffled softly. The mare shook her head and leaned toward Mercedes.

"She's glad to see me," Mercedes informed O'Grady.

"Time for a reunion later. We have to put distance between us and this place."

Mounting, O'Grady led the way. He set their pace at a fast trot.

"What spies are you talking about?" Colonel Judson Kilgore demanded icily.

"The—ah—a—ah—woman, sir. A woman and the man she was with," Eddie stammered out to his father.

"How did they get into town? More, how did they get into the officers' mess, and at a time when a new campaign was being announced?"

"Well, ah, sir, I—ah—we found the woman." He went on to describe the hunting party's discovery of Mercedes in a camp obviously occupied by two people and what went on afterward.

"Didn't you have enough local sluts to go jiggity-pokey with?" Colonel Kilgore snarled.

"This one was different, sir. She looked good. A real beauty."

"A goddamn spy. What else? What about the man?"

Eddie haltingly described the encounter with O'Grady. He concluded with his discovery that the two had fled.

"Christ!" Colonel Kilgore exploded. "Was it absolutely necessary that I be saddled with an idiot for a son? There is no newly promoted man named O'Grady, there has never been an O'Grady in this company. And, having found this pearl beyond price, whatever possessed you to give her away to someone of lesser rank?"

"I—well, I . . . I—er, that is, sir, I find dalliance with pros—er—ladies of faded virtue to be somewhat distasteful, sir," Eddie responded stiffly.

Colonel Kilgore snorted derisively. "I'd not be surprised to find that you found 'dalliance' with anyone of the female persuasion distasteful."

"Father! Er—ah—sir, I consider that remark totally uncalled-for."

"What is uncalled-for is bringing two spies into our midst and allowing them to escape. Orderly!" he bellowed.

A straw-haired, moon-faced youngster in blue tunic and trousers popped into the room. "Sir!"

"Fetch Cap—Major Means. I want him here at once."

"Yes, sir."

"While we wait, Edward, tell me some more. Are you sure this man was an American?"

"Oh, yes, sir. He had flame-red hair, spoke with a—ah—it's hard to describe. Pennsylvania accent, I suppose, with a bit of Irish lilt."

"Then his name might well be O'Grady," Colonel Kilgore speculated aloud. "Which means that . . . that the government . . ." He broke off abruptly and paced the floor. "No. That can't be. They could never get away with sending troops down here after us. Relations are too delicate between the U.S. and Mexico. So he couldn't be a contract scout." A crafty light came into the colonel's eyes.

"But he could be a spy. That clever, arrogant civilian bastard, Johnson, isn't above sending someone to spy on us, provide information to the enemy that could be damaging. O'Grady heard the announcement of a new campaign?"

"I have to assume so, sir. He and the girl were, ah, up there in the, ah, pleasure rooms. It's obvious now they weren't doing what is usually done there."

"How would you know about that, you bloody eunuch?" Colonel Kilgore growled.

"Sir! Again I must protest. I'm not a eunuch, I'm not unnatural."

"Oh? Then what is it makes your pecker stiff, boy? You certainly haven't been acting lately like a man with balls."

"I beg to differ, sir. I did come directly here to inform you, sir, and to admit my having been duped." Eddie drew himself up and sucked in a deep breath. "Think of it, sir. That took considerably more balls than many in this company have."

Colonel Kilgore turned back to his son, a bemused expression lighting his face. "By God, you're right, son. You're right about that."

Major Means knocked and entered. "Sir, you sent for me?"

"Yes. We have a problem, Lance. Captain Kilgore here will fill in the details later. There's a pair of spies, a man and a woman. The woman is Mexican, the man an American, or at least of European origins. They may know too much about our intended plans. With this silver shipment coming, I need every man. As you know, there are Mexican troops guarding it. We can't send out a large search party to recover the spies. I want you to pick three good men from among our original complement. Have Captain Kilgore describe the fugitives to them and send them on the way. We can detail one Mexican guide to go along. Now, both of you hop to it."

Stiffening to attention, Means and young Kilgore saluted. "Yes, sir."

"And, ah, Eddie," Colonel Kilgore added as an aside to his son, "if they recover the spies, all will be forgiven. If not, *sczzzzzzit!*" Eyes locked on his son's, he slowly drew a finger across his throat to emphasize his meaning.

Pale bands of white and pink lined the eastern horizon when Canyon and Mercedes halted for the second time. A screen of feathery tamarisk hid them from the road.

"We'll have to rest the horses," O'Grady explained.

"What about feeding them, and us?"

"The horses, yes," O'Grady agreed. "We can wait."

"For how long?"

"Until we get well beyond the patrol area for Kilgore's troops."

Mercedes' face softened. Moisture enlarged the pupils of her eyes and she blinked back tears. "Canyon, I know I thanked you for coming after me. But that was hardly enough. I am so grateful, so eternally in your debt. I . . . I know now what you meant about staying out of the action. I was foolish to insist on coming so near to these evil men."

"It's all right. You're safe and so am I. Look at it this way. It's a good thing this happened before Miguel got here. His honor would have demanded he do something dramatic and totally useless in an attempt to rescue you. Stealth, I have often found, pays off where flamboyance can only get a person dead." An impression, a scrap of information that had nagged him all night finally clicked into place.

"Kilgore is calling up his entire outfit. Something big, at least something worth drawing on a lot of firepower, is going on. One of Kilgore's officers speculated on it being the spring silver shipment. It could be. Or maybe it's Miguel and all those who have joined up with him."

"I pray it is," Mercedes stated hopefully, hands clasped together. "If it isn't, what shall we do? And . . . and where are we going now?"

O'Grady had been thinking on that question most of the night and answered quickly, the corners of his mouth lifted in a partial smile. "Why, to the Johnny Rebs, of course."

16

Goss, Heller, and Dunn sat their mounts under the wide-spread limbs of an ancient oak. They listened attentively as Jesús Pintaro described what he had located. Starlings quarreled noisily in the branches above, making the Mexican guide's garbled English even more difficult to understand. When he concluded, Goss eyed him narrowly.

"How certain are you of this?" the hatchet-faced renegade corporal asked.

"En absoluto, cabo," Pintaro answered earnestly in Spanish. "Absolutely," he repeated in English. "The spies have not left the high road. They are only a little more than two leagues ahead of us."

"Is there any shortcut we can use to catch up to them, Chuy?" Goss asked, using the diminutive of Pintaro's first name.

"Alas, no, Cabo Goss." He produced a wicked smile. "But if we keep riding into the night, we can reach them before the moon rises."

"Uh—when'll that be?" Dunn asked.

"A little after midnight," Pintaro responded.

"Then that's what we'll do," Goss decided. "We'll catch those bastards and wring them dry, then bring their heads back to the colonel."

Long slanting orange rays heralded the approach of sundown. Reluctantly O'Grady called a halt. He could see the strain their escape and flight had put on Mercedes. Urgent as his desire was to reach the road into the Confederates' valley, he had to admit they needed the rest.

It had been near midnight when they escaped from Villadolor. After picking up the packhorse with their gear, O'Grady and Mercedes had ridden through the night and all the next day until now. Short rest periods for the horses had not been enough for man or beast.

"What can you stir up to eat without lighting a fire?" he asked Mercedes.

She made a face, then forced a tired smile. "There are some tamales and tortillas, of course. They would taste better warm, but we can manage."

"Wrap them in my saddle blanket after I strip it off Cormac," he suggested. "I learned that from some Indians once. They do that while they ride to soften jerked buffalo meat."

While Mercedes fussed with their meager meal, O'Grady fashioned a low lean-to of fresh branches, backed against the large bowl of a gigantic bristle-cone pine. It would keep the dew off during the night. Mercedes came over and arranged their blanket rolls into one comfortable double bed. She produced an inviting smile that left no doubt as to her intentions. O'Grady approved; his own thoughts ran in the same direction.

O'Grady's Indian patent served to restore some pliability to the simple fare, though not quite reaching body temperature. Washed down with fresh cold water, it at least was filling. Darkness had fallen by the time they munched the last crumbs. Conversation had been sparse and O'Grady's words sounded loud in his ears.

"We'd better get some sleep," he suggested.

"Oh, yes, let's get in bed," Mercedes gushed, then ended in a little gasp. O'Grady could sense, if not feel, the blush that rose to her cheeks. Easy enough to take care of. He reached out and drew her into his arms. Their lips met and sampled each other eagerly. Mercedes sighed. O'Grady chuckled and cupped one of her firm palm-size breasts. Clothing rustled and Mercedes turned back the top blanket. Naked, they embraced again and experienced the building warmth of their passion.

"Hurry, Canyon," Mercedes murmured. "I . . . I need you so badly."

O'Grady eased her to the comfort of their bed. His hands explored her body. Caressing gently, he sought out the sensitive spots that would send her to greater heights of arousal. Mercedes found his rigid member and began to fondle it. Playfully she tweaked it and circled its girth with thumb and one finger. O'Grady kissed her pert nipples, licked them. One finger traced the line of her jaw.

With his other hand he sought the fevered triangle at the junction of her thighs. She cooed with delight when he cupped her mound and kneaded it gently. Shivers of delight ran up her lithe torso. O'Grady kissed her navel. Mercedes squirmed. Deftly he ran a finger along her cleft, parted it, sought out the responsive node at the top. Mercedes gasped. For long, happy minutes they continued to touch, and rub, and squeeze.

"Now, Canyon, oh, hurry, now," Mercedes pleaded.

"Patience, Mercy, patience. We've only begun," O'Grady whispered to her.

"I . . . I c-can't stand it."

"Oh, yes. Yes, you can. I'm going to take you where you've never been before. Let go and enjoy."

Mercedes became a dynamo of unbridled stimulation. She quivered, gulped, sobbed, moaned, writhed, and clung to O'Grady. His own ardor grew in proportion to hers, racked his body with crashing waves of sensation. Rising in a moment of incredible ferment, Mercedes sprawled on top of him. With a gasp of desperation she scrambled down his lean, hard frame. Opening wide, she took O'Grady's manhood deep within her mouth.

Her lips encircled him, closed and caressed. Flickering like a teasing flame, her tongue worked miracles of titillation. Now it became O'Grady's turn to groan and pulse with ardor. His hips flexed, drove his ample endowment deeper. Mercedes squealed around it and kept up her powerful, tugging pressure. They began a tangle of waving limbs, passion-sweated torsos, and blind eyes that saw only love.

When O'Grady came close to convulsing into completion, Mercedes removed herself and whirled to bring her face close to his. "Now? Surely now, Canyon, now-now-now."

"Y-yes," he managed shakily.

Mercedes swiftly slid backward, straddled his hips, rose and positioned her fevered cleft, then brought her body downward. He penetrated her with ease, sliding partway before the impetus of her impalement lagged. Mercedes grinned down at him in the starlight. Slowly, ever so languorously, she relaxed and accepted more of his pulsing organ.

"Ah, Mercy, Mercy, what did I ever do before you?" O'Grady panted.

"Probably quite well, you goat. You've ignited a fire within me I never knew existed. I can never quite settle for a mere mortal again."

"You put me in rarefied company, *mecushla*," O'Grady bantered back. "Best that I know, I've not changed my residence to Olympus as yet."

"Olympus? Wh-what is Olympus?" Mercedes grunted in query as she raised and lowered herself, driving him deeper within her palpitating passage.

"Another time. I—aaah! Oh, my . . . my, so good, so . . . so fine," he praised as new skyrockets of delectation went off in his groin.

Mercedes began to rock and O'Grady joined the rhythm. True to his prediction, they both reached new heights of fantastic joy. When the ultimate had been achieved once, she cased him tightly, a second cataclysmic release built over long, ecstatic minutes. At last they tumbled into soft, fuzzy contentment.

" 'And one beamy smile from you/ Would float like light between/ My toils and me, my own, my true/ My dark Rosaleen!/ My fond Rosaleen!' Ah, like most Irish poems, 'tis a story of sadness, but it has its light moments," O'Grady murmured in her ear.

"You're different, Canyon. You are unlike any man, or boy, I've ever known. Even my father, who enjoyed whimsy as a release from the demands of business, never reached the flights of fancy that you call up with ease."

"I take it that's a compliment. For which I give you grateful thanks. The moon will rise in a little while. By its light we'll make slow, soul-healing love."

"You promise me?"

"That I do." O'Grady started to add more, but a slight sound, the snap of a twig, silenced him.

Instantly alert, he put a finger to Mercedes' lips. She responded with an understanding nod. O'Grady's hand slid toward the holster that held his Colt Army model. It might be nothing, a prowling animal, only he didn't think so.

"There they are, all in a heap," Dunn whispered to Goss. "Musta been humpin'."

"Quiet," the corporal breathed back.

"It's gonna be their last hump," Dunn went on, ignoring the admonition.

"It'll be the last of you if they hear us coming. Spread out, we'll take 'em from three sides."

Silver light edged into the valley as a fat moon glided above the surrounding peaks. Trees became hard black silhouettes, the ground seemed dusted with diamonds. The dark forms lay still to the eyes of the hunters. Cautiously they spread apart and waited for some unspoken signal. Dunn and Heller fingered their rifles expectantly. Goss fisted his revolver. On the south side of camp a horse stamped a hoof in boredom. The trio of deserters froze.

Ten yards behind Goss, Jesús Pintaro stifled a nervous gulp. He had never done anything quite like this. An owl's querying hoot jangled his tenuous composure. He felt sweat break out on his forehead. Ahead he saw the three gringos move forward. Another few paces and they would be out of the trees. Jesús had no intention of being exposed and vulnerable in that clearing. He hugged a big hemlock at the edge of the open space. Goss and his two men took three rapid steps onto bare ground.

Faster than sound, the twin yellow-orange winks of muzzle blast reached Pintaro's eyes before he heard the shots or saw Heller fall sideways into the dirt and Dunn go to one knee.

"Christ!" Corporal Goss blurted. "How'd they know?"

He had no time for more oral speculation. Triggering a round, he dived to the left, rolled, and began to crawl toward the trees. Jesús Pintaro cringed back into the forest. Goss halted his frantic crawl when he heard Dunn's rifle crack to life. He turned back and added his own firepower to the contest. Two more shots punished the silence from the direction of the camp.

"Yiieee! I'm hit. Hit again," Dunn wailed. He swayed wearily and started to sag. Another .44 ball smacked into his chest. With a soft grunt, he fell dead.

Angry at the desertion of his friends, goaded by fear channeled into relentless rage, Corporal Goss rose to his feet and charged the camp, his discharging six-gun lighting the way with muzzle flash. He made it to Dunn on the last round. Holstering his revolver, he grabbed up the rifle beside the dead man. Swiftly he cycled two rounds through the Spencer, into space no longer occupied by their intended targets.

From off to his right he saw the wink of a fired weapon.

Then Corporal Goss saw nothing at all. The ball that killed him ripped into his throat, severed the carotid artery, and splashed out the back. He bled to death in five powerful heartbeats.

"Canyon? My God, Canyon, are you all right?" Mercedes cried from her position behind a thick pine trunk.

"That I am."

"Who are they? Why did they come at us like that?"

"I'd judge they came from Kilgore. They'll not trouble us anymore, though."

"I—ah—I got one of them," Mercedes said faintly.

"That you did, *mecushla*. Drilled him right into hell." O'Grady showed himself, went about quickly checking the corpses.

"I—oh—I feel . . . feel sick," Mercedes moaned a moment later.

"Go ahead and get it over with. 'Tis a shock the first time you help a man out of this life. Then we might as well move on. There'll be no more sleepin' here tonight."

Her stomach voided, Mercedes stepped into the open, O'Grady's shirt draped around her bare shoulders. She looked drained and used-up. O'Grady felt instant sympathy for her. She had no business being here, taking such risks. Then she spoke.

"Nor any more loving by moonlight," Mercedes declared wistfully.

"Saints preserve us," O'Grady exclaimed in an exaggerated tone. "I think you'll come through the ordeal all right, if that's what you have on your mind."

Neither of them heard the cautious, stealthful retreat of Jesús Pintaro. He suddenly found pressing need to return to his former home in Concepción del Oro, far to the south in Nuevo León. He also found himself quite unwilling to deliver such terrible news to Coronel Muerte.

Light mist filled the wide, pleasant valley of Leesberg. Canyon O'Grady reined in, with Mercedes at his side. They showed the strain and soil of their last hours on the trail. Uncharacteristically, Mercedes' chin drooped and she sat hip-shot in the saddle. O'Grady had a fine coating of dust on his clothing and more made a flat sheen of his exposed skin. Both were red-eyed with fatigue.

"There it is, Leesberg," O'Grady said unnecessarily.

"Do you really think they will help, *corazón*?"

"I expect to find out soon enough."

They rode directly to the city building. The chill and impending rainstorm had driven most people indoors, yet a gaggle of children formed in their wake. O'Grady dismounted and helped Mercedes from her mare. Two of the older boys dashed forward to take the reins and secure the horses to an iron ring held in the extended hand of a cast-iron statue of a small black boy. O'Grady peeled out of his trail-grimed linen duster and left it across the saddle. From one bag he removed a folded envelope and put it inside his jacket. Inside they were shown, with only the slightest of delays, into the office of Mayor Anson Stilwell.

"Mr. O'Grady, Miss Fernández, I had not expected to see you again so soon," Stilwell greeted, showing them to comfortable chairs across the desk from his seat.

"We have a problem," O'Grady began bluntly.

"Ah! Is it that you have found this Colonel Death?"

"Indeed. Unfortunately we located him in the fortified city of Villadolor."

Stilwell frowned. "That is a most serious circumstance. If I may speak bluntly, and without the usual circumlocution of Southern politicians, suh, I would say you would have a hell of a time rooting him out of there."

"That's why we came to you for help," O'Grady said levelly. "I consider the circumstances somewhat different, revealing this to you, sir, as opposed to doing the same to a Mexican official." He removed a wrinkled buff envelope from his inside jacket pocket and handed it to Anson Stilwell. "Read this."

Stilwell did, frowned, reread the first two paragraphs. "I understand that you are an agent of the President of the United States. The letter makes that quite clear. What, however, put it in your mind that any of us would aid the Yankee cause, no matter who asked?"

"I'm fully aware of your feelings toward the United States, particularly its army. Yet I wonder if you or the other ex-Confederates in this valley hold any liking for a Yankee officer, a deserter and murderer, bent on plundering your part of Mexico?"

Silence lay heavily over the room. O'Grady could hear the ticking of a Regulator mantel clock, the click and whir of its gears as the minute hand advanced. Anson Stilwell bit his lower lip, chewed at it in reflection. The examination of his conscience took nearly a full minute more. As the big black arrow pointed to the next slash mark on the clock face, Stilwell drew a deep breath.

"No. We found peace here, and the opportunity to live our lives in the manner to which we were accustomed. We owe our Mexican neighbors for that freedom, and we owe it to our posterity to ensure continued peace and tranquility. All I need do, Mr. O'Grady, is summon my friends and neighbors. They'll fight to the man, I'm sure of it. Considering the menace this Colonel Kilgore represents to everyone, I'm equally certain the Mexican government will prove generous in their gratitude, once we've eliminated him."

Stilwell had the bell in the town hall rung, soon joined by the church tocsin, and that of the volunteer fire department. Men and boys from fifteen to forty began to assemble in the open square in front of the city hall. Before long fifty of them, all heavily armed, stood in a loose semblance of ranks. When the question was put to them, they responded with a rousing cheer. Orders were given for every man to prepare himself. They would march out at dawn the next day. After the volunteers had been dismissed, Anson Stilwell spoke quietly to Canyon O'Grady.

"We—ah—have a little something we liberated from some Yanks in Texas that might help turn the battle in our favor, O'Grady. If you'll come with me."

He led the way to a low, inconspicuous building, which turned out to be a respectable armory, half of it underground. Stilwell made a wide, sweeping gesture with his arm.

"Look around you. There, cases of blasting powder. Fuses and caps in that cabinet. Those are cases of .45-70 ammunition." They extended from floor to ceiling along two walls.

"What good are they?" O'Grady asked, confused. "There are only a few Springfield rifles converted to take cased ammunition, all in the hands of U.S. troops."

"Quite true, Mr. O'Grady. But that ammunition also fits . . . this," Stilwell went on as he whipped away a large tarpaulin, revealing a Gatling gun.

Gleaming brass and polished nickel winked in shafts of

sunlight entering the barred, slit windows. O'Grady stared openmouthed, then cleared his throat.

"By all that's holy. That thing could cut down a regiment."

"As some of them damn nearly did several times during the closing days of the war," Stilwell answered bitterly. "I don't think it would be misplaced using it against Kilgore and his horde."

"Nor do I," O'Grady answered, his mood bordering on awe.

17

A band, made of those too young or too old to ride out with the expedition and a few youthful girls, assembled on the green outside the city hall in Leesberg early the next morning. The former Confederates began to form ranks as the music struck up.

They rendered "Dixie" with fervent gusto. Then "Aura Lee." When Anson Stilwell gave the command to form a column of threes to the right, the band struck up a new tune. At once the men in ranks began to sing.

> We are a band of brothers
>   And native to the soil.
> Fighting for our heritage
>   We won by honest toil.
> And when our rights are threatened,
>   To fight we do prefer.
> Hurrah for the Bonnie Blue Flag
>   That bears that single star!

A Confederate battle flag broke out at the head of the column. Caught by the wind, it snapped out straight and proud, gold-fringed, blood-red field, white cross, and the thirteen stars of the Confederacy. The sight moved even O'Grady.

Once more in his uniform of a lieutenant colonel in the Confederate States Army, Anson Stilwell rose in his stirrups and brought up his gauntleted right hand. "For-waard, at the trot . . . Yooo!"

Some of the women shed tears. All waved and cheered. The small children raised patriotic pandemonium. At Stilwell's gesture, O'Grady and Mercedes joined him in the vanguard.

Stilwell smiled in obvious appreciation of his return to command, so that the saber scar on his right cheek seemed a live, mobile thing. "Sergeant Glenndower, I will hold you personally responsible for the young lady's safety. She is to be taken to the rear in the event of any hostile action."

"Yes, sir, Colonel. Uh—beggin' the colonel's pardon, sir, but is this duty mine because I have a wife and three kids back on my farm?"

Stilwell looked him straight in the eye and spoke without any expression, though his clear blue orbs held a mischievous twinkle. "Certainly not, Sergeant. It's because you're an expert marksman and I want to keep you out of the direct line of fire in order that you have time to employ yourself as a sharpshooter to take out their officers at your leisure."

"Oh, very good, sir, thank you, sir." Glenndower saluted smartly and turned toward Mercedes. "And my wife will thank him too."

Trailing a plume of dust, the scout rode back to the gray-clad column. He hailed the point with a shout and the signal was given for a halt. Showering pebbles and clods chest-high on his horse, he reined in and saluted Lieutenant Colonel Stilwell.

"Troops, sir. Mexican regulars. Just around this bend."

Stilwell frowned. This was one thing he had hoped to prevent. No doubt the Mexicans would not be pleased to find another armed force of Northerners at large in their mountains. He looked left and right, to where high bastions of the range prevented turning aside and going unseen. The other alternative would be to turn back, retreat into their valley. His shifting glance took in Canyon O'Grady.

"Pardon, sir," the scout injected, "but they're headed our way at a good clip."

"Well, O'Grady? What would you suggest we do?"

"It was bound to happen sooner or later. The government had to send troops. Why not meet them head-on, tell the officer in charge that you were on your way to offer services in helping to rid the countryside of the bandits."

"It couldn't hurt. And it might work. Adjutant, have the sergeants pass the word for the men to stand easy."

In a fraction over ten minutes, the Mexican banners rode into view. Fully a third of the unit came into sight before the column halted. A series of complicated bugle calls rang in the air. Green-white-and red uniforms shimmered in the sun reflected off copious quantities of shiny golden chains and braid. Three men detached themselves from the head of the column and rode toward the Americans.

They halted at a distance of fifty paces. Their posture, and a regal nod of the head by the apparent leader, indicated that they found this encounter most disconcerting. There they sat their mounts and glowered at the representatives of the American group.

Their obvious intent for a parley had sent Major Grant Monroe, Lieutenant Buell, and Sergeant Pickering forward. They rested easy now, by appearance, though tight lines around their eyes betrayed their strained vigilance. The decorated and gold-braided Mexican officer rapped out a sharp question.

"Señor Coronel, we are citizens of Mexico, loyal to the government of Benito Juárez," Monroe said in liquid Spanish.

"Where do you reside?" snapped the colonel.

"In the Valle del Sol, Señor Coronel."

"Why are you wearing those uniforms?"

Monroe formed a deprecating expression. "They are the only uniforms we have. We were riding to offer our services in fighting the Yanqui bandits and must wear something to identify ourselves from our enemy."

A younger officer, to the left of the colonel, leaned toward his superior. "It is known there is a large armed force of gringos loose in these mountains, Coronel. Here we see a large armed force of gringos in uniform. Isn't it obvious that these are the freebooters we have been sent to punish?"

"Umm. A good point, Teniente."

"Then I suggest we strike now, while they are unprepared for a battle."

"Your idea has merit, Lieutenant. Yes, I think it most likely that if we eliminate these gringos we will be rid of our bandits."

While the colonel worked himself up to giving the order to attack, a civilian detached himself from the Mexican column and trotted forward. He looked beyond the parley group and studied the gray uniforms of the opposing troops.

"Coronel," he spoke respectfully, "we know that a large number of hill bandits have joined the outlaw Yanquis. Also certain imperialists. If these are the enemy we've been sent against, where are those men? Could they be waiting in ambush? I think not."

"What do you mean, *señor*?" the colonel asked.

"These are the uniforms of the Confederacy, not the Yanqui army. I believe what this officer said." He looked again at the head of the Confederate column and his eyes widened. "In fact, I am positive of it. You will notice a young woman with the vanguard, Coronel? That is my *prima*, Doña Mercedes Elena Fernández y Obregón. I am certain of that. She has sworn to kill this Coronel Muerte and I don't think she would be riding with him. Shall we ask?"

To the colonel's grudging question, Major Monroe responded in the positive that it was indeed Señorita Fernández. She and an American had come to Leesberg to ask for help against Colonel Death and his band. Colonel Méndez sighed and shook his head. At his signal the lancers came forward. He made a curt announcement of this and Monroe rode back to advance the Confederates.

In a relaxed atmosphere several of the Confederates produced copies of their citizenship papers. Mercedes and Miguel had a loud, joyful reunion, after which he explained what had happened to him.

"There were so many of them, Canyon," he said, referring to the volunteers from communities raided by Kilgore. "The more that came with me, the slower we had to move. Then we came across these troops and I thought it a good idea to join forces."

"Yes. Now we have them here, what do we do with them?" O'Grady asked rhetorically.

"I'm afraid that will be up to the colonel. He's newly promoted and, ah, somewhat jealous of his position of command."

"Then we'll talk with him," O'Grady suggested.

Colonel Méndez drew himself up, chest out like a pouter pigeon's, when O'Grady asked if the company of lancers would be accompanying them to Villadolor to attack the garrison force while the bulk of Kilgore's troops were in the field. "*Señores*, my primary mission is to provide additional escort for a silver shipment from Durango. After that, I am at liberty to pursue the outlaw force.

"Will that silver train pass nearby to Villadolor?" O'Grady asked.

"Certainly. Right in front of there. In fact, we will probably spend the night there," Colonel Méndez answered stiffly.

"Not unless we get it out of the hands of the outlaws you speak of," O'Grady countered.

"What?" the colonel exploded.

"Coronel Muerte, Colonel Judson Kilgore, has taken Villadolor. He has strengthened the fortifications and three nights ago rode out with the main complement of his force, a unit about two companies in strength. I can't be certain that their target is the silver shipment, but I'm willing to bet it is."

A wild gleam of battle lit Colonel Méndez's eyes. "Then we shall smash them once and for all. They can have no idea of our presence in the area. Surprise will deliver them into our hands."

"You may find that you have more than a handful," O'Grady responded dryly. He considered it obvious that no appeal would influence the ambitious colonel. He turned to Miguel. "Will your detachment stay with the army or come with us?"

"With you, amigo," Miguel answered promptly. "I see it too. Together we can take Villadolor. That deprives Coronel Muerte of a base of operations."

"Exactly," O'Grady clipped, warming to a fresh idea. "Colonel Méndez, we'll take our leave of you, then, to plan our own course of action. May you have the best of luck engaging Kilgore."

"*Buena suerte, también,*" the colonel answered absently, already drafting in his head his report to the War Office in Ciudad México.

Once the Confederate column had reformed, augmented now by the forty or so men Miguel Fernández had accumulated, Canyon O'Grady held a council of war with him and

Anson Stilwell. "Miguel said it a minute ago. Here's a chance for us to steal a march on Kilgore. The more I consider it, I'm positive that madman will strike at the silver train. There's no other reason he stripped the town of nearly every one of his men."

"Do you think we can take Villadolor easily?" Anson Stilwell asked.

"We should be able to. We'll use Miguel's men, with some sort of ruse to get inside town, then take it. That'll create an ideal situation. Kilgore's men will be out in the open, caught between the Mexican forces, your Confederates, Anson, and the fortified town."

"I wouldn't want to be in his place then," Stilwell said. "We're with you on this. Now, why don't we put some distance between us and those lancers?"

"My thought exactly," O'Grady approved.

"Lord God, they're all dead." One of Kilgore's advance scouts bent low over the bloated corpses of the men sent to deal with the spies.

"Ain't no sign of anyone doin' any bleeding, 'sides them," his partner remarked as he searched the former campsite.

"Damn. We better get back and tell the colonel. Wonder what happened to that Mezkin guide that rode with 'em?"

"Dead too, or lit out to save his skin," the other opined. "The colonel ain't gonna like this."

He didn't, they soon learned after rejoining the column. His ice-gray eyes grew cloudy and seemed to stare through the bearers of bad news, through the mountain peak beyond, and far into another world. He ran long spatulate fingers through his gray-shot black hair and worked his mouth as though trying to rid himself of a foul taste. At last he sighed and slapped his swagger stick against one thigh.

"Once we have the silver, we'll deal with this impostor officer and the Mexican whore. Damned spies. Mark my word, gentlemen, all will not be as it seems. This deadly pair will turn out to be far more than the surface appearance indicates." It was not prescience, but deep-seated feelings of persecution, that led Judson Kilgore to the correct assumption. "They are government agents, sent from Washington City to put an end to my affairs."

*   *   *

Evening found the combined force of Mexican vaqueros and townsmen and the Confederates encamped less than ten miles from Villadolor. The ground around appeared familiar to O'Grady, and he settled in to discuss their options once they reached the community.

"I've changed my mind about your people infiltrating the town, Miguel. It might appear more believable to whoever Kilgore left in charge for a small force of, say, fifteen gringos, and Rebs at that, to seek to join up with the bandit army. Once inside, they can neutralize the cannon, open the gates, and we will ride in."

Anson Stilwell and Miguel Fernández considered the new plan. "Sounds reasonable," Stilwell agreed.

"Yes, we would be suspect as having come from the army," Miguel accepted.

"Well, then, with that decided, we can work out details of seizing Villadolor from the inside."

They talked on while savory odors began to fill the mountain air. Both parties had brought along fresh food and skilled cooks. By the time the plan had been refined, the meal was ready. O'Grady discovered another anomaly when the troops lined up to eat.

Unlike Union officers he had encountered during the dark days of the Civil War, the Confederate officers refrained from taking their meals until all the men had been served. He commented on it and Stilwell explained.

"In the early days, most officers had personal servants along and dined alone or entertained friends. When food and other rations ran short, we all began to share equally so that everyone got at least something or went hungry together. We've kept the practice out of habit."

"An admirable one, by my lights," O'Grady complimented. "Nothing lightens a man's burden more than to see his privations shared by everyone."

With the presence of so many, her cousin Miguel in particular, Mercedes and O'Grady mutually agreed that any thought of passion must be put aside. He spent a lonely, chill night rolled in blankets to one side of the caisson that bore the Gatling gun. At dawn hot coffee, fresh biscuits, country ham, and red-eye gravy came out of the kitchens of the Confederates, with tortillas, a hominy-and-tripe stew, and beans for the vaqueros. An hour after their awakening, the allied company set off toward Villadolor.

To their disappointment, the gates of Villadolor had been tightly shut against any entry or exit. From a place of concealment, O'Grady studied the sentries on the battlements through a pair of brass-cased field glasses. Though they looked fairly alert from a distance, the close-in view showed lines of fatigue and boredom. Too few guarding too much, with only short rest periods between duty hours.

"They certainly show a military background," Anson Stilwell remarked.

"Yes," O'Grady agreed. "Look closer, though. This won't last long," he predicted. "Those men are bored and tired. Their vigilance will begin to slip soon, if it hasn't already. For the present, it prevents our taking the town easily, as we outlined. I suggest we take a small detachment and start off along the road west. Never know what we might turn up."

18

Miguel Fernández was left in charge of the larger portion of the combined force, which would wait and keep Villadolor under observation. On a whim, Lieutenant Colonel Stilwell ordered the Gatling gun brought along with the twenty men selected to accompany him and Canyon O'Grady. On the well-maintained road they made good time. By nightfall the advance scout reported back that they had visual contact with the caravan of wagons bearing silver from Durango. Well off the highway, they made camp behind a stand of pines.

Dawn came with a brief rain shower. Thin and chill, the drops rattled down on the camp, then swept away in less than fifteen minutes. Everyone breakfasted and mounted, the scouts suggested a route through the pines toward a promontory from which they could observe the high road and the approach of the caravan. Seasoned horsemen all, the Confederates negotiated the uphill course with ease.

"From here we can . . . Oh-oh, look." Anson Stilwell pointed toward the road.

A column of horsemen swung into view from the direction of Villadolor. They spread out and concealed themselves among the rocks and trees. It took no effort at speculation to realize that Colonel Kilgore had beaten them to the silver shipment. From the size and position of the mad colonel's troops, it was obvious that it would be impossible to warn the unsuspecting Mexican wagon train.

"Perhaps a shot, fired at the right moment," O'Grady considered aloud.

"You were thinking of warning them also," Stilwell pointed out.

"Damn little chance. There come the advance scouts," O'Grady declared. "Odds are Kilgore will let them go right on by."

"I feel helpless, watching while this happens. We should warn the scouts."

O'Grady shook his head. "It would only get them cut down and the wagons attacked anyway."

Bobbing heads of mules appeared at the crest of the grade. The first wagon would soon come into sight. O'Grady could almost feel the tension of the ambushers waiting below. He squinted his eyes against a suddenly revealed sun and watched one after another of the heavily laden vehicles glide deeper into the trap. When the first came abreast of the far end of the waiting outlaws, rifle fire ripped apart the quiet of the morning.

At the lead wagon, the draft animals dropped to their knees, shot in their traces. At once the same happened to the rearmost conveyance. Instantly puffs of smoke appeared along both sides of the road. Mounted brigands dashed out of the trees, raking the lancer escort with rifle and revolver fire. Men screamed and died, or fell wounded all along the caravan. Trapped in this narrow, steep portion of the road, the additional force of Colonel Méndez's lancers proved useless to hold off the horde.

More men died, and a couple of mules. O'Grady felt sick at being a helpless witness to such wanton carnage. He should have anticipated it, after all; hadn't he said this would be where Kilgore struck? Confined between the high walls, jammed in with the soldiers and wagons, their own force would have fared no better. Knowing that didn't make it any less bitter a lesson. Slowly the firing dwindled.

O'Grady counted some nine of Kilgore's men down, several pierced with lances. A few of the demoralized lancers and several drivers had surrendered. They stood helpless in the road, hands above their heads. Voices could not be distinguished from their distance, yet O'Grady had no doubt when Kilgore—it had to be him in the blue garrison hat and black plume—gave the order to shoot them down.

They died in a roar of gunfire, screaming and begging for mercy. Only one cursed their murderers, standing defiantly to take one ball after another. O'Grady recognized Colonel Méndez. The colonel wrenched a small revolver from his boot and shot a blue-uniformed sergeant between the eyes. Another fusillade ripped into him and he flopped onto the ground.

At once Kilgore gave a signal and horse handlers trotted out of the trees with fresh draft mules to replace the slain ones. Men turned their mounts over to other riders and assumed places on the wagons once the harness had been fitted. With the dead animals replaced, the army of brigands set off in the direction of Villadolor.

"Well, we don't have much of a chance against them, sitting here," O'Grady said with disgust. "They'll move slowly because of the weight of that silver. There must be ten thousand bars in those wagons."

"What do you suggest, considering that?" Stilwell asked.

"We stay ahead of them, keep them in sight while we have scouts pick out a proper place to lay our own ambush. Good thing you brought along that Gatling gun. It should work nicely to even the odds."

"We're going to fight them? Just twenty of us against that many?"

O'Grady produced a grim smile. "You're damned right we are."

Twelve miles beyond the pass where the silver train had been captured, the terrain widened out into an oval valley, pinched in its middle like an hourglass, and narrowed to high mountain walls at each end. East of the waist stood a goodly screen of trees on the north slope. At Canyon O'Grady's suggestion, Lieutenant Colonel Stilwell placed fifteen of his cavalrymen in among the thick growth of pine and hemlock. The other five served as a screen for the Gatling-gun crew. They effectively corked the eastern end of the valley.

Stilwell saw the strategy at once. If half of the enemy force could be cut off between the pinched middle and the far end of the valley, that would mean fewer troops to deal with at one time. Likewise, if his small force was compelled to disengage and withdraw, not all of the enemy could come at them at the same time.

"Like Mosby," Stilwell reasoned to O'Grady. "Hit a few, cause a lot of damage and move out, to come back and hit them again."

"Right," the government agent acknowledged. "A highly mobile, determined smaller force can always inflict maximum losses on a larger, unwieldy complement."

"Cold camp tonight and no noise," Stilwell suggested.

"Right on that too. Come tomorrow, when half of that silver train gets to this side of the hourglass, we slash through them, rip up the vanguard with the Gatling, and pull back. Before next evening we should be able to get in at least one more ambush against what's left."

Kilgore put his men on the trail before dawn. Only the squeal of protesting wagon wheels gave advance warning when they reached the western end of the little valley. A single picket put out there to watch for the approach came riding back with the hasty news. At once the men made ready. O'Grady had to admire the lack of restlessness and prebattle jitters among the seasoned Confederate fighting men. They went about the business of killing with calm deliberation. Good. Right now he needed that.

"They're coming," Anson Stilwell whispered beside him.

Where the rock formations pushed out toward each other, O'Grady could discern solid black shapes, darker than the night. Behind them came the squeal of a protesting axle. To O'Grady's right he caught a thin slice of intense white along the sawtooth ridge of mountain peaks. The figures approaching them grew more distinct. Pale rose followed the initial brightness.

"Keep coming," O'Grady whispered to himself.

Several wagons could now be seen against the background of lingering night. The entire east had become washed in gray. Orange and vermilion shot columns into the sky. O'Grady could see the features of the nearest bandits. They seemed small and pinched at this distance. He shook himself out of immobility and started off toward the far end of the valley.

Greater brightness, blotted here and there by large clouds, streamed out of the east. O'Grady could see the individual blades of grass. He turned right and covered the short leg to the low brush that masked the Gatling gun. Still Kilgore's men advanced into the deadly snare. Another hundred yards. Then fifty. Two of the outriders and the lead wagoner perked up with the coming of daylight and increased the pace. Four—five—six, half of the wagons had come beyond the pinched waist.

"Whooo—eeee! Whoooo—eeeee-hooo—eeeee—hooo!" The haunting Rebel yell echoed through the valley.

"Yeeeeeeee—aaaaaaaah—hoooooo!" came the reply from the Gatling crew.

With a softer pat-pat-pat than he had expected, O'Grady heard the Gatling open up. Mules screamed and collapsed in their traces. A horse reared, took two .45-70-450 slugs through the breast, pitched the rider, and fell on top of him. The other lead horse whinnied in terror and jerked to the right.

It put the man in the saddle in line with the revolving barrels of the Gatling. One thumb-sized round punched through the man's leg and into his mount's belly; the next three stitched upward, effectively cutting the outlaw in half vertically. Turning the crank, the gunner traversed, spraying bullets across the line of wagons and drivers. A bugle chirped from the tree line and fifteen troopers charged down on the stalled caravan.

Judson Kilgore had a sudden unreasoning belief that he had been transported in time. Once more he heard the blood-jelling barbarian Rebel cry and saw the terrible gray line thundering down on him. It was Bull Run all over again. He wanted to scream, to run, hide, get away from the terrible death in the hands of Jeb Stuart's cavalry.

"What is it? Who's that?" a rattled voice shouted at him.

"It isn't real, it can't be," Kilgore denied. He closed his eyes, shook his head. When he looked again, the Confederates, battle colors streaming, still charged down on him. He gripped his nearly frayed reason.

"You, trooper, bring up the men." To the teamsters and escort he gave brisk orders. "You men stand fast. Take careful aim. There can't be many of them. Move up!" he bellowed to the seven troopers with him.

With the wagons halted, the mounted outlaws pressed forward. A clot of half a dozen burst past the mounds that obstructed the battlefield. Kilgore turned to them, pointed to the charging Rebels.

"Go after them, meet them head-on," he commanded.

Suddenly the Gatling stopped, the barrels obstructed with powder fouling. Cursing, the gunner and his three assistants stripped away the magazine, grabbed up a bucket of soapy water, and doused the hot breech. The liquid sizzled and bubbled a moment, then ran free, changing from milky-colored to jet black. One man took another bucket and more soap mixture to the muzzle and began swabbing out the barrels.

"Only trouble with these things. The powder isn't clean-burning enough. The gun always fouls up after a few dozen rounds."

"How long to get it ready?" O'Grady asked.

"Two, three minutes, if we're lucky."

"Keep at it."

Out in front the battle swayed one way and then the other before O'Grady's eyes. Without the menace of the Gatling gun, mounted troopers streamed through the narrows, intent on driving off their foe. O'Grady soon saw that Kilgore's foresight still worked well. Fresh animals were hastily hitched into the harness by makeshift means and the wagons turned around. A heavy rear guard formed. Kneeling in the dust, they drove off the inferior force of gray cavalry. O'Grady wanted to be out there in the thick of it, giving a few good knocks of his own. He settled for taking careful aim and shooting a sergeant off his saddle.

Through the dust and powder smoke, O'Grady located Judson Kilgore. He moved like a man possessed. Never resting, the renegade colonel went everywhere, shouting encouragement, firing at the gray-clad soldiers who attacked their flank.

Under increasing pressure, the Confederates had to withdraw. When recall sounded on the bugle, the men lifted a lusty cheer. It only served to further disconcert the deserters and misfits who served with Kilgore. Two long, tense minutes later, the Gatling gun opened fire again.

"Back! Back! Pull back," Kilgore's voice could be heard shouting over the tumult.

No longer able to drive off their attackers, Kilgore's divided force had but one choice: to withdraw. The Gatling harassed them, the cavalry harried them. Stilwell commanded well.

His men would swoop in, discharge a volley into the retreating outlaws, and ride off again before return fire could be registered. Whirling away, they would come in at another angle.

"Keep pressing, keep in there," Stilwell shouted over the rattle of gunfire.

Kilgore established a strong rear guard and set men to lash the wagon teams back through the gap. Two rigs with dead teams could not be taken along. He cursed foully as he disappeared beyond the hillocks. Again the Confederate bugler sounded recall.

"Form up and we'll pull out," Lieutenant Colonel Stilwell ordered.

"Excellent work, Colonel," O'Grady congratulated the powder-grimed Reb. "We'll find another place and hit them again."

"I've taken casualties. We'll have to send ahead for reinforcements. There's too many of them for this small a unit."

"They're off-balance," O'Grady protested. "Now's when we have the advantage."

"These men have wives and families. I have a responsibility to them as well," the big blond Confederate objected.

"Men who died in towns from Chihuahua to here had families too. Some of those families died with them," O'Grady answered hotly. "My country's honor rests on this. The President wants Kilgore out of Mexico one way or the other. I intend to damn well do what he asks. If you want to pull off and wait for reinforcements, do so. I'm asking for volunteers to come along and take Villadolor away from Kilgore. Do what you can to harass him along the way and I'll see you in Villadolor."

19

A sudden rattle of gunfire broke the grim silence that hung over Colonel Judson Kilgore's column of renegades. A pistol ball moaned past Kilgore's ear and he flinched involuntarily. In the ranks behind him he heard a man cry out as a bullet from a hidden sniper found meat.

Wounded in the shoulder, the young Mexican bandit complained volubly while his companions tried to quiet him. Kilgore's anger rose as he looked around for the source of the harassment. To his left, Sergeant Gruber pointed toward a dissipating smudge of powder smoke.

"Over there, Colonel," the flinty noncom said through tension-thinned lips. "And there . . . there . . . and there. Must not be many of 'em."

"You're right, Sergeant, or they'd attack in force."

"How much longer do we have to put up with this?" Captain Edward Kilgore complained as he rode forward from his position with the second platoon.

"Get back to your men," Colonel Kilgore snapped. Then his expression softened somewhat, recalling how his son had placed himself in the way of a hidden marksman and risked death to protect his father. "I imagine we'll be faced with harassing fire all the way to Villadolor. Frankly, son, I don't know where these Rebel scum came from, or why they are attacking us, yet they are, and there's little we can do about it."

"Why, sir?" Edward asked, outraged by the close-to-constant ambuscades.

"These silver wagons slow us down, we outnumber them, and for some reason, they are determined to do us harm. My suspicion is that they want the bullion for themselves."

Already the squad sent out to ride down the concealed shooters had turned back to the column. Having found no enemy, they returned without even firing a round to relieve

158

their stress and frustration. Father and son, the Kilgores
watched them approach in tight-lipped silence.

"We outnumber them, sir," Edward prompted. "If we
could only send men ahead to locate these ambushes and
eliminate them."

"If we did that, we'd lose the men. *They* would then
outnumber those we sent. Like it or not, we have to live
with it."

"Call it the luck o' the Irish," Canyon O'Grady offered
in jest. "Looks like those lads did our work for us."

From their vantage point in a screen of crowded pines,
O'Grady and three of Anson Stilwell's Confederates looked
toward the main gate of Villadolor. It stood open, unat-
tended, with no visible sign of sentries on the battlements
above. The three cannon appeared abandoned by any crew.
Faintly, the sounds of music and singing came from beyond
the wall.

"What do we do now?" a young Reb asked.

"You ride back and bring up half of the troops. I'll take
a dozen men and get inside town."

A fleeting frown gullied the youth's brow. "Hadn't we
ought to wait for Colonel Stilwell?"

"Not when we have an opportunity like this," O'Grady
informed him.

Ten minutes later, O'Grady and twelve gray-uniformed soldiers cantered up to the gate. A somnolent sentry roused
himself enough to come to his feet and challenge the new
arrivals.

"Who goes there?" he asked in a dull voice.

"The man who's going to put you on the retired list,"
O'Grady answered as he leveled his Colt on the guard's
forehead. "Don't anyone act brave," he addressed the other
two sentries, "and no one will get hurt."

In seconds they secured the gate. At once O'Grady and
seven men pushed on into Villadolor. Behind him, the huge
gates swung closed and men swarmed up onto the banquette. Smiling brightly, O'Grady led the way to the Edificio Municipal.

"Who the hell are you?" a bored sentinel demanded.

"The man who's going to let you live if you lay down
that rifle and don't make any noise," O'Grady responded.

Swiftly the troops with him secured the city hall. Few of

the skeleton force remaining in Villadolor realized that the town had been captured out from under them. The majority continued their past few days' routine of pleasure-seeking. That ended an hour later when a shout from the wall brought the gate open and twenty-five Confederates and half of Miguel Fernández's men rode into Villadolor. Much to O'Grady's disapproval, Mercedes came with them.

"You shouldn't be here," he said shortly.

"Why not? I've a right to see that murderer destroyed."

Impatience stamped O'Grady's face. "Our thirteen took on twenty-five of theirs, half of them drunk, and that's no victory. You could be killed in the fighting when Kilgore gets here. He's got nearly a hundred and fifty men with him."

Mercedes stamped one small foot. "I'm staying," she answered him hotly. "There's less than half the men left at camp, and your Colonel Kilgore is out there. Where would I be safer?"

O'Grady chose not to answer, and turned from her to speak to the mixed force that had ridden with her. "Now, that was nicely done," O'Grady complimented his allies. "All we need do is wait for Kilgore and his troops to return."

Everything looked normal when the vanguard of Kilgore's renegade army rounded the buttress of granite that blocked the view of Villadolor. The gates were tightly closed, according with his orders when the main force departed to take the silver shipment. Men walked the parapets and more crewed the three cannon. When they rode closer, he saw to his consternation that the Mexican flag flew from the jackstaff atop the city hall. At five hundred yards' distance, a puff of smoke blossomed at the muzzle of one cannon.

"What the hell are they shooting for?" Major Lancelot Means demanded rhetorically.

"Why are they shooting *at us*, is what you should ask," Kilgore responded acidly.

With an eerie ripple, the ball passed overhead and its charge exploded back among the loaded wagons. Screams of men and animals followed. The middle cannon had been trained around and fired now, its deadly projectile bursting the moment it struck the ground a bit to the left of the column.

"Form line of attack," Kilgore bit out, knowing they had but one choice.

Quickly the troops deployed. The bugler sounded the charge and one hundred and thirty yelling men raced toward the walls.

"They're going to do it anyway," one of Miguel's vaqueros shouted down from the wall. "There's sure a lot of them."

Quickly the cannon crews depressed their tubes and, at three hundred yards, fired loads of canister. A dozen golf-ball-size round shot, neatly stacked on their wooden pallets, whizzed through the air and burst apart at two hundred yards. Seven men and horses, then four more, tumbled in the dirt. The cries of the wounded could be heard over the din. Firing as they came, the renegade army closed rapidly. Once more the barrels lowered to bring the attackers into range.

With swift efficiency the crews reloaded, grapeshot this time, and fired all three artillery pieces. Blood, dust, and powder smoke filled the air. Along the walls the few Confederates and Miguel's Mexican volunteers opened fire. Mortal accuracy broke the charge. Kilgore's troops swirled a moment in confusion, then rode hastily out of range. Over the distance separating them, O'Grady heard the mad colonel's shouts.

"I want every man this time. Spread out. Give them more air than meat to shoot at. De Vega, take your section out toward the drop-off and then cut in for the gate."

A sudden thought took O'Grady from the wall. In the livery stable he retrieved his long metal-bound case and opened it. From it he took the Berdan telescope rifle and a dozen rounds. At a trot he returned in time for the next charge.

"There's more of them than before," one astonished Confederate informed O'Grady as he climbed to the banquette.

"I don't like to say this, but we might not be able to hold the wall."

"What if we can't?"

"We fall back to the inner wall and fight from there."

With that simple explanation out of the way, O'Grady rested the long barrel of the Berdan on the parapet and sighted in. Seeming larger than life, Hernán de Vega's chest filled the circular field. O'Grady set the cross hairs on a button and squeezed gently.

With a sharp report, the Berdan fired. A moment later, O'Grady saw the imperialist fly out of the scope's field. He felt a moment's satisfaction while he opened the breech and slid in a new cartridge. For a second he held Judson Kilgore's face in the sight, took up slack, and started his final squeeze. A rifle bullet smacked into the stone block beside his head.

Reflex jerked him backward and triggered the rifle. Tortured air alone felt the bullet's passage. Cursing his misfortune, O'Grady loaded another round. By the time he sought the malignant colonel, the charge had broken and the renegades had sped away.

"He'll wait now," O'Grady anticipated. "Maybe ten minutes, maybe half an hour."

Miguel Fernández appeared at his side. "I've lost three men. Those men might be renegades and bandit scum, but they sure know how to shoot."

"It's more than tricky to fire accurately from the back of a galloping horse," O'Grady informed him. "Likely it's luck more than skill."

By midafternoon Kilgore had made two more abortive attempts to take the wall. Each charge took a toll of the defenders, though, and he grew aware that the volume of fire had slackened. Major Means remarked on that while the troops made ready for another try.

"There aren't as many people holding the town as we thought, and the number's been reduced in the last two attacks."

"Yes," Kilgore agreed. "Only it doesn't solve our problem of taking Villadolor. I'd estimate we outnumber them better than three to one. But without siege machines we haven't much chance of breaching the walls."

"Then why don't we build some? At least scaling ladders."

"See to it, Lance. Put the slightly wounded to work on ladders and maybe a ram. If we could rig up a wagon some way . . ."

An hour later, six riders, volunteers who knew they had little chance of surviving the task, tested the bite of their ropes. Attached to the tongue of a silver wagon, the lines would be used to pull the heavy vehicle toward the main gate in the wall around Villadolor. Atop the load of silver ingots, a huge tree trunk had been lashed in place. The pointed butt end extended beyond the tongue, which had been tied to it. When all was in readiness, Colonel Kilgore gave the signal to form a double line of skirmishers and the entire force moved out.

Slow to yield at first, the wagon gained speed steadily until the horses drawing it reached a shambling gallop. Bullets sang around the six volunteers, who hugged low on the necks of their mounts. Incredibly, they had crossed three-quarters of the distance between the bend in the road and Villadolor before one man cried out from a wound in his left shoulder. He hung on desperately and spurred his mount until he drew blood.

"Yeeee—iiiiii!" a short, stocky Mexican bandit wailed as the gateway loomed large in front of him. A slug punched a hole through the wide, upturned brim of his sombrero and penetrated the crown. It burned scalp on its way to exit the rear of the hat.

Eyes watering from the sudden hot pain, the bandido choked off his exuberant yell and wiped furiously at the tears. A moment later he and his companions released their ropes and the lumbering wagon hurtled forward on its own.

It struck the gate with a thunderous hollow boom. Driven by inertia, the ponderous weight bulled through the restraint of drop bars, and wood splintered loudly. At once a cheer rose among Kilgore's troops. Pressing their luck, they swarmed toward the breach.

Their elation served to drown out a distant bugle call.

"We have 'em in our grasp," Anson Stilwell observed enthusiastically.

"Sure enough, Colonel," his adjutant responded. "Caught between us and the wall. No time like the present, suh."

"Sound the charge," Stilwell commanded.

Brassy notes spilled into the air. Thin and keening, the Rebel yell followed, growing in volume to a roar as the mounted Confederates rushed down on Kilgore's suddenly demoralized troops. An answering wail came from the wall. A rippling volley spurted from the attacking Rebels, to fill the dusty space around the renegades with deadly bees.

Shrieks of anguish rose from the milling men around the

damaged gate as a huge caldron of boiling water tipped over
the battlements above and cascaded over them. Enfiladed
fire ripped into them from the crenels between sturdy granite merlons. In moments the demoralized renegades took
the shock of Anson Stilwell's cavalry.

Revolvers flashed yellow-orange and sabers twinkled in
the sunlight. Relentlessly the Confederates hacked their way
through the panicked horde. Men and horses screamed in
anguish. From the wall, Canyon O'Grady looked down on
the battle with a sinking feeling of helplessness.

How he wanted to be in there, to come face-to-face with
the man he had been sent to destroy. A heavy cloud of dust
and burned powder obscured the conflict for several long
moments. O'Grady fumed while the gunfire slackened, then
ended. Unnatural as the ferocious letting of blood, the
silence that ends all battles hung over the combatants.

The spell lasted only a moment, and then the cries of the
wounded and dying rose to haunt the weary minds of the
survivors. All about, renegade soldiers, bandits, and imperialists raised their hands in surrender. Moaning men cried
out for mercy. Canyon O'Grady sucked in a great draft of
air.

"Well, then, by God, it's over. Open the gates," he commanded loudly. "I want to find Kilgore."

20

She had to be somewhere. He had seen her on the battlements through his field glasses before the first attack.
Edward had seen her too, and pointed out the female Mexican spy to him.

"That's her," Edward Kilgore had told his father, his
voice hollow with chagrin. "I'll give odds we'll find that red-
haired bastard with her."

"How did she get inside?" Colonel Kilgore asked.

"Maybe she never left," the young captain speculated.

"Whatever the case, she must be partly responsible for the city being recaptured. When we take it back, I'll have her hanged."

Those words mocked Colonel Judson Kilgore now. In the midst of the most furious fighting, after the gate had been breached, he had stripped off his distinctive Mexican jacket and sombrero and insigne of rank and wormed his way under the silver wagon. From there he had entered Villadolor unobserved.

His intention was to find the red-haired American—he'd seen him on the wall also—and the Mexican woman and kill them. His great design lay in ruin. Not given to excessive optimism under the best of circumstances, Judson Kilgore weighed his losses and his chance of success in getting revenge and decided he had a chance.

Cold gray eyes clouded with his suppressed rage, his bushy brows knitted in a scowling face, he proceeded through the town, determined to avoid capture. At least, he told himself, until he did for that Mexican slut and the American spy. Then he would worry about how he might get out of town.

Deep frown lines marred Canyon O'Grady's high clear brow as he stalked back into Villadolor. Judson Kilgore's body had not been among the littered dead outside the wall. Nor had he been among the prisoners. Neither had the body of his son been identified. O'Grady considered the possibility that they had escaped past the Confederate and Mexican force that had attacked them from behind, but rejected it. More likely, he reasoned, the mad colonel and Edward had entered the town in search of some refuge.

"You men," he directed a dozen gray-clad idlers, "Colonel Kilgore and his son are not accounted for. Search the area between the outer wall and town." O'Grady gave them descriptions and sent the men on their way. He would check the wall himself.

His search proved fruitless and he headed into Villadolor. Logically, O'Grady reasoned, Kilgore would head for the center of the town or perhaps the pottery works on the far side. He might succeed in getting out that way. Eyes alert, the government agent headed for the Plaza de Armas.

* * *

Mercedes fumed inwardly. Canyon had sent her into the town when Colonel Death's men attacked the first time. She could shoot as well as any man. Why had he not let her exact revenge for her family? Well, her thoughts directed her, it was over now. It would be proper to offer thanks for the destruction of the enemy. Thus directed, she crossed the gardenlike center of the plaza and started up the steps to the cathedral. A hissing voice, heavy with malice, stopped her.

"So . . . I found you, bitch."

Mercedes turned to find herself facing Colonel Death. He held a Remington service revolver in his hand, the muzzle pointed at her middle. His thin bloodless lips had drawn back, revealing crooked yellowed teeth.

"I . . . I'm only a woman," Mercedes depreciated herself, thinking fast.

"You are the one. You are responsible for the loss of my command."

Mercedes paled as his finger whitened on the trigger. "No—no. I'm a woman, from this town. I'm . . . I'm nothing to you."

"You lie," Kilgore spat, hard and low in tone. The muzzle of his six-gun rose toward her face.

Canyon O'Grady stopped abruptly. There before him, not fifty yards away, he saw Judson Kilgore. Far too close for comfort, Mercedes stood beyond the defeated yet vengeful colonel. From this angle, he dared not shoot. Only a slight error, or an air inclusion in one of his cast bullets, perhaps some other defect, could send the slug crashing into Mercedes.

"Kilgore. Judson Kilgore," O'Grady called out.

Cat-quick, Kilgore whirled, his Remington leading the way. "Who are you?"

"My name's Canyon O'Grady."

"You're the spy!" Kilgore shouted, his voice breaking.

"I'm not exactly a spy. President Johnson sent me here to bring an end to your insane bloodbath. It appears I've accomplished that."

Fear-induced paralysis left Mercedes and she quickly mounted the steps to the porch. The minute she cleared his field of fire, O'Grady loosed a round. His bullet cut through shirt cloth in Kilgore's left armpit. Rattled by the near-miss,

Kilgore discharged his revolver hastily, and plowed ground near O'Grady's feet.

O'Grady sent another bullet toward Kilgore, who darted diagonally across the lower steps. The hot lead screamed off a stone riser. Immediately O'Grady fired again. Another miss, that cracked past an inch in front of Kilgore's nose.

It caused him to reverse directions. As he did so, he raised the Remington and squeezed the trigger. The hammer fell on a spent cap. A second later, O'Grady discovered he had expended his last round. Already Kilgore had holstered his weapon and rushed at O'Grady with his saber drawn.

Keen-edged steel swished through the air above O'Grady's head as he ducked the first attack. Kilgore doubled back and hacked downward. The heavy blade clanged loudly when O'Grady parried the blow with his revolver barrel. He pivoted to one side to avoid Kilgore, and his left hand sought the coffin-shaped handle of his sheath knife. His fingers circled it and closed securely as Kilgore bore in again.

Once more O'Grady blocked the slash that would have split his head from crown to chin. While Kilgore's weight still pressed the sword against Colt steel, O'Grady swung with his bowie knife, intent on burying it in Kilgore's stomach. Suddenly the resistance against O'Grady's gun hand ceased as Kilgore spun to his left, away from the threatening blade. Off-balance, O'Grady sprawled forward.

"You're mine now," Kilgore shrieked, gobbets of spittle foaming at the corners of his mouth.

O'Grady righted himself barely in time to avoid a downward chop of the saber. It clanged on the lip of the plaza's fountain and O'Grady kicked at the side of Kilgore's head. Stunned by the savage blow, Judson Kilgore lost his grip on the weapon and it fell into the water. He turned, left hand pawing at the handle of a belt knife.

A soft grunt came from O'Grady as he swung his bowie. Kilgore sucked in his gut and jumped backward a step. When his feet came down, he lunged with his own blade, missed, and started a desperate run toward the cathedral steps. O'Grady came after him.

Hidden in the untended grass of the plaza park, a small stone turned under Canyon O'Grady's foot and sent him sprawling. Kilgore howled in triumph and turned back on him. The flat crack of a small-caliber revolver discharging silenced his gloating. Bone, cartilage, and blood blew out the front of his left trouser leg.

Pain washed his face alabaster and he crumpled, his kneecap shot away. Beyond him Mercedes stood at the head of the stairs, a smoking .36 Colt Navy held competently in both hands. O'Grady took a step forward as, from his prone position, Kilgore drew back his arm and threw his knife.

O'Grady staggered as the tip bit into flesh below his rib cage. Thrown without full force, only a third of the blade penetrated his side. He looked down at it a moment before he took another step and bent down toward Kilgore.

Wincing at the pain, he swung his bowie in a wide arc. The keen edge bit into Judson Kilgore's shoulder, slashing deeply before it met bone. In the same moment, the gun fired again and cloth jumped on Judson Kilgore's right leg, as Mercedes blew off his other kneecap. He cried out wretchedly before the darkness of unconsciousness closed over him.

O'Grady winced as he pulled the knife from his side. He used a neckerchief to stanch the thin flow of blood and stepped around the stuporous body of Judson Kilgore. "Thanks," O'Grady panted, looking up at Mercedes. "I needed that." Then he struggled to produce a lopsided grin. "I don't mean that the way it sounds."

"You've been hurt," the lovely young Mexican blurted.

"You were very brave," O'Grady countered. "Where'd you get that pistol?"

"My purse. I've carried it all the way from Castaños."

"You picked the right time to use it."

"Now . . . Canyon, is it over now?" she asked in a little-girl voice.

"Not quite. Edward Kilgore, the one with the greasy black hair who brought you here, is still on the loose. We'll find him, though."

"Then what?"

"I take the Kilgores, father and son, along with those army personnel who deserted with them and survived the fighting, back to my country to hang."

"And I'll go with you, *corazón*," Mercedes hastened to say.

"Looks like you have your man," Anson Stilwell declared

as he walked up, forestalling any remark from O'Grady about taking Mercedes along.

"That I do. It would be me lying there if it hadn't been for Mercedes."

Stilwell looked from one to the other and at the unconscious Kilgore. "Young lady, you are surely wicked with that popgun," he observed ruefully.

Canyon O'Grady turned fully to the Confederate and extended his hand. "I have to give you my thanks, and gratefully so. Sorry to say I can't do more right now. Though I'm willing to bet that when I inform the President of your aid, you ex-Rebs might well find a changed climate should any of you wish to return to the United States."

"That's all well and good, my friend," Anson Stilwell admitted. "But first we have a fall crop to tend and a harvest to get in. Then there's the new schoolhouse to build." He stopped suddenly, conscious he had started to ramble and to talk like a man with his future already decided.

After securing all of the prisoners, the men from Valle del Sol mounted and rode off for home. Edward Kilgore had not yet been located. Squads of Miguel Fernández's volunteers scoured Villadolor for him, while others cleaned up after the battle and dug a large mass grave for the dead among Kilgore's men. Canyon O'Grady had one of the town's doctors tend to his wound, and those of Judson Kilgore, and then locked the mad colonel in a stout cell of the Villadolor jail. He and Mercedes stood in the plaza looking at a community gratefully returning to normalcy.

"It is a beautiful place, no?" she asked him. "Maybe, after we take Coronel Muerte and the rest back to your country, we can come here to live?"

Surprise registered on O'Grady's face. "Woah, now, lass. I'm not entirely free to do as I wish. I've responsibilities to my job, and . . . and—ah—I'm not the marryin' kind."

Mercedes produced an impish smile. "Who said anything about marriage?"

"You're forever amazing me, darlin'," O'Grady said with spirit.

He opened his arms wide and she came to him. A moment later she stiffened and gave out a soft cry. Overriding her gasp, O'Grady immediately heard the gunshot. Mercedes went limp as he lowered her to the ground.

"Edward, you bastard!" O'Grady shouted.

Another round whipped past his head and rang loudly
when it struck the fountain. O'Grady released Mercedes,
conscious that she was severely wounded. He fisted his
reloaded Colt Model '60 and darted toward the front of the
cathedral. A puff of powder smoke betrayed the hidden
sniper's position in the belfry as he loosed a third round. It
scarred a granite step in front of O'Grady and whined off
into the distance. Then O'Grady hit the central portal and
bounded into the narthex.

Silence filled the holy place. O'Grady pushed through
stained-glass doors into the nave. At the head of the aisle,
just past the chancel rail, the body of Father Antonio Pérez
lay sprawled in front of the altar in a pool of blood. The
cold rage at Edward Kilgore's cowardly act of back-shooting
Mercedes magnified now with the murder of a harmless
priest.

O'Grady turned back to the narthex and to his right,
through a narrow door that gave access to the north tower.
He took the winding stairway two risers at a time. Halfway
up, the trapdoor above him opened and Edward Kilgore
fired wildly. Three fast unaimed and ineffective rounds
emptied the Spencer the young Kilgore held and he sobbed
with desperation.

"I'm inclined to kill you here and now," O'Grady
growled. "But I'll take you back with your father to hang."

"You'll never take me," Edward shrieked.

In panic he flung the rifle away, in hopes of hitting
O'Grady. It clattered harmlessly down the tower and
O'Grady came on. Edward had lost his revolver somewhere, and, trapped high in the tower, on the bell floor, he
howled in rage and terror. His tantrum ended, though,
when O'Grady came through the square opening in the
floor.

"You bastard," he gulped. O'Grady produced a sneering
laugh.

Edward leapt at him, hands clawed to scratch and gouge.
O'Grady lifted one arm, wincing at the pain the movement
caused in his side, and popped Edward with a short, hard
right. Staggered, Edward reeled backward until he hit the
largest bell and slid down its concave waist to the flaring
strike ledge. He forced himself to stand as O'Grady closed
in.

Hands fumbling at his waist, Edward got to his feet in

time to dodge O'Grady's fury-driven fists. The younger man backpedaled a moment until his pistol belt came free. With the tip wrapped around his hand, he swung the heavy U.S. buckle like a medieval flail. It seethed through the air, snaking in sinuous curves like a bullwhip. When he got the speed to where he wanted it, Edward lashed it out toward O'Grady's face.

Raising his left arm, his teeth biting his lip to suppress the flaming pain in his side, O'Grady used a boxer's block. The oval buckle caromed off his forearm and struck a small bell to O'Grady's left. It rang in high pitch, quickly faded, while Edward sought to return the belt for a second blow.

"Keep away from me," Edward wailed, putting his shoulder into the cast of the belt.

This time O'Grady missed a complete block and the heavy pewter buckle slammed painfully into his chest. Instantly Edward yanked the belt back and the leather snapped behind his head. He started to hedge to his left, flicking the murderous improvised weapon.

"Go away. Forget about me," he pleaded. "Leave me alone."

"They're going to stretch your neck, you little twit," O'Grady snarled.

The big letters grew rapidly larger as the buckle hurtled at O'Grady's eyes. Again he blocked. This time the leading third of the belt wrapped around his wrist. Seizing the leather with his fingers, O'Grady planted his feet and gave a solid yank. Edward bounded toward him, unable or unwilling to let go of his only means of defense.

O'Grady hit him in the mouth. Edward's lips mashed, teeth broke. Groaning and spitting blood, Edward ducked his chin to protect his face, raising his left arm in an ineffectual block. O'Grady hit him again, and again.

Knees sagging, Edward suddenly realized his opponent no longer held the belt. He gave it another figure-eight whip forward and back, then forward again. O'Grady ducked low and reached for the two-inch-wide strip of leather. He gave it a hard grasp and pulled until his knife wound shrieked in agony.

Edward Kilgore came off his feet. He hurtled through the air, hands spread wide and flailing. The belt fell away, yanked again by O'Grady. Edward kept moving. He tilted downward and dropped through the open trapdoor. He immediately began to scream. His hands fought bell ropes to find a purchase and stop his long plummet to the floor so far below. In so doing he got his head tangled in one and jerked suddenly to a neck-breaking halt.

A long moment of silence followed. Then the deep-throated peal of a huge bell rang out in the tower. Panting from exertion, O'Grady bent over the hatchway and watched Edward Kilgore's twitching body ride up and down as the bell rocked on the great wheels attached to its crown. Heavy lead weights attached to the stock kept the bell in motion.

O'Grady pushed back his hat and made an observation to the unhearing dead man. "I told you I'd see you hang."

Slowly he descended, avoiding the corpse, then rushed outside the cathedral and over to where Mercedes lay on the grass. He knelt at her side and a moment later her eyelids flickered open.

"I hurt terribly," she said faintly.

"Well you should. You've been shot in the back." He raised her slightly and felt around the blood-wet area of the entry wound. "It must have been an underpowered round, one of those like we found they were making in that little shop. I can feel the bullet stuck in your shoulder blade. It's serious, but not deadly. You'll soon be well again."

Mercedes tried to smile. "Oh, I'm so glad. But what about you? Will you be going away right now?"

O'Grady gave that some thought, surprised at the direction his reflections took him. "I don't think so. First I'll take you home and nurse you back to health. Then I can run these vermin up to the border. And along the way, lass, while you're healing," he added, "we'll find the time to love away all memory of this terrible time."